## Iris:
*Message*

Magician Pierce Atkins had a lot of tricks up his sleeve—and he needed all his skill in magic to get his message across to skeptical Ryan Swan. But a message of love has a powerful magic all its own....

# NORA ROBERTS

### LANGUAGE OF LOVE

**Love has a language all its own, and for
centuries, flowers have symbolized
love's finest expression.
Discover the language of flowers
—and love—
in this romantic collection of 48 favorite
books by bestselling author Nora Roberts.**

# NORA ROBERTS

### LANGUAGE OF LOVE

## THIS MAGIC MOMENT

*Silhouette Books*®

SILHOUETTE BOOKS
300 East 42nd St., New York, N.Y. 10017

THIS MAGIC MOMENT © 1983 by Nora Roberts.
First published as a Silhouette Intimate Moments.

Language of Love edition published September 1991.

ISBN: 0-373-51024-1

# Chapter One

He'd chosen it for the atmosphere. Ryan was certain of it the moment she saw the house on the cliff. It was stone gray and solitary. It turned its back on the Pacific. It wasn't a symmetrical structure, but rambling, with sections of varying heights rising up here and there, giving it a wild sort of grace. High at the top of a winding cliff road, with the backdrop of an angry sky, the house was both magnificent and eerie.

Like something out of an old movie, Ryan decided as she shifted into first to take the climb. She had heard Pierce Atkins was eccentric. The house seemed to testify to that.

All it needs, she mused, is a thunderclap, a little fog and the howl of a wolf; just some minor special effects. Amused at the thought, she drew the car to a stop and looked the house over again. You wouldn't see many like it only a hundred and fifty miles north of L.A. You wouldn't, she corrected silently, see many like it anywhere.

The moment she slid from the car, the wind pulled at her, whipping her hair around her face and tugging at her skirt. She was tempted to go to the seawall and take a look at the ocean but hurried up the steps instead. She hadn't come to admire the view.

The knocker was old and heavy. It gave a very impressive thud when she pounded it against the door.

Ryan told herself she wasn't the least nervous but switched her briefcase from hand to hand as she waited. Her father would be furious if she walked away without Pierce Atkins's signature on the contracts she carried. No, not furious, she amended. Silent. No one could use silence more effectively than Bennett Swan.

I'm not going to walk away empty-handed, she assured herself. I know how to handle temperamental entertainers. I've spent years watching how it's done and—

Her thoughts were cut off as the door opened. Ryan stared. Staring back at her was the largest man she had ever seen. He was at least six foot five, with shoulders that all but filled the doorway. And his face. Ryan decided he was, indisputably, the ugliest human being she had ever seen. His broad face was pale. His nose had obviously been broken and had reknit at an odd angle. His eyes were small, a washed-out brown that matched his thick mat of hair. Atmosphere, Ryan thought again. Atkins must have chosen him for atmosphere.

"Good afternoon," she managed. "Ryan Swan. Mr. Atkins is expecting me."

"Miss Swan." The slow, barrel-deep voice suited him perfectly. When the man stepped back, Ryan found herself fighting a reluctance to enter. Storm clouds, a hulking butler and a brooding house on a cliff. Oh, yes, she decided. Atkins knows how to set the stage.

She walked in. As the door closed behind her, Ryan took a quick glimpse around.

"Wait here," the laconic butler instructed and walked, lightly for a big man, down the hall.

"Of course, thank you very much," she muttered to his back.

The walls were white and draped with tapestries. The one nearest her was a faded medieval scene depicting the young Arthur drawing the sword from the stone, with Merlin the Enchanter highlighted in the background. Ryan nodded. It was an exquisite piece of work and suited to a man like Atkins. Turning, she found herself staring at her own reflection in an ornate cheval glass.

It annoyed her to see that her hair was mussed. She represented Swan Productions. Ryan pushed at the stray misty blond wisps. The green of her eyes had darkened with a mixture of anxiety and excitement. Her cheeks were flushed with it. Taking a deep breath, she ordered herself to calm down. She straightened her jacket.

Hearing footsteps, she quickly turned away from the mirror. She didn't want to be caught studying herself or attempting last-minute repairs. It was the butler again, alone. Ryan repressed a surge of annoyance.

"He'll see you downstairs."

"Oh." Ryan opened her mouth to say something else, but he was already retreating. She had to scramble to keep up.

The hall wound to the right. Ryan's heels clicked quickly as she trotted to match the butler's pace. Then he stopped so abruptly, she nearly collided with his back.

"Down there." He had opened a door and was already walking away.

"But..." Ryan scowled after him, then made her way down the dimly lighted steps. Really, this was ridiculous, she thought. A business meeting should be conducted in an office, or at least in a suitable restaurant. Show business, she mused scornfully.

The sound of her own footfalls echoed back at her. There was no sound at all from the room below. Oh, yes, she concluded, Atkins knows how to set the stage. She was beginning to dislike him intensely. Her heart was hammering uncomfortably as she rounded the last curve in the winding staircase.

The lower floor was huge, a sprawling room with crates and trunks and paraphernalia stacked all around. The walls were paneled and the floor was tiled, but no one had bothered with any further decoration. Ryan looked around, frowning, as she walked down the last of the steps.

He watched her. He had the talent for absolute stillness, absolute concentration. It was essential to his craft. He also had the ability to sum up a person quickly. That, too, was part of his profession. She was younger that he had expected, a fragile-looking woman, small in stature, slight in build, with clouds of pale hair and a delicately molded face. A strong chin.

She was annoyed, he noted, and not a little apprehensive. A smile tugged at his mouth. Even after she began to wander around the room, he made no move to go to her. Very businesslike, he thought, with her trim, tailored suit, sensible shoes, expensive briefcase and very feminine hands. Interesting.

"Miss Swan."

Ryan jolted, then swore at herself. Turning in the direction of the voice, she saw only shadows.

"You're very prompt."

He moved then, and Ryan saw that he stood on a small stage. He wore black and blended with the shadows. With an effort, she kept the annoyance from her voice. "Mr. Atkins." Ryan went toward him then, fixing on a trained smile. "You have quite a house."

"Thank you."

He didn't come down to her but stood on the stage. Ryan was forced to look up at him. It surprised her that he was more dramatic in person than on tape. Normally, she had found the reverse to be true. She had seen his performances. Indeed, since her father had taken ill and reluctantly turned Atkins over to her, Ryan had spent two entire evenings watching every available tape on Pierce Atkins.

Dramatic, she decided, noting a raw-boned face with a thick, waving mane of black hair. There was a small scar along his jawline, and his mouth was long and thin. His brows were arched with a slight upsweep at the tips. But it was the eyes under them which held her. She had never seen eyes so dark, so deep. Were they gray? Were they black? Yet it wasn't their color that disconcerted her, it was the absolute concentration in them. She felt her throat go dry and swallowed in defense. She could almost believe he was reading her mind.

He had been called the greatest magician of the decade, some said the greatest of the last half of the century. His illusions and escapes were daring, flashy and unexplainable. It was a common thing to hear of him referred to as a wizard. Staring into his eyes, Ryan began to understand why.

She shook herself free of the trance and started again. She didn't believe in magic. "Mr. Atkins, my father apologizes for not being able to come himself. I hope—"

"He's feeling better."

Confused, she stopped. "Yes. Yes, he is." She found herself staring again.

Pierce smiled as he stepped down to her. "He phoned an hour ago, Miss Swan. Long-distance dialing, no telepathy." Ryan glared before she could stop herself, but his smile only widened. "Did you have a nice drive?"

"Yes, thank you."

"But a long one," he said. "Sit." Pierce gestured to a table, then took a chair behind it. Ryan sat opposite him.

"Mr. Atkins," she began, feeling more at ease now that business was about to begin. "I know my father has discussed Swan Productions' offer with you and your representative at length, but perhaps you'd like to go over the details again." She set her briefcase on the table. "I could clarify any questions you might have."

"Have you worked for Swan Productions long, Miss Swan?"

The question interrupted the flow of her presentation, but Ryan shifted her thoughts. Entertainers often had to be humored. "Five years, Mr. Atkins. I assure you, I'm qualified to answer your questions and negotiate terms if necessary."

Her voice was very smooth, but she was nervous. Pierce saw it in the careful way she folded her hands on the table. "I'm sure you're qualified, Miss Swan," he agreed. "Your father isn't an easy man to please."

Surprise and a trace of apprehension flickered into her eyes. "No," she said calmly, "which is why you can be sure of receiving the best promotion, the best production staff, the best contract available. Three one-hour television specials over three years, guaranteed prime time, with a budget that ensures quality." She paused only for a moment. "An advantageous arrangement for you and for Swan Productions."

"Perhaps."

He was looking at her too closely. Ryan forced herself not to fidget. Gray, she saw. His eyes were gray—as dark as was possible without being black.

"Of course," she continued, "your career has been aimed primarily at live audiences in clubs and theaters. Vegas, Tahoe, the London Palladium and so forth."

"An illusion means nothing on film, Miss Swan. Film can be altered."

"Yes, I realize that. To have any impact, a trick has to be performed live."

"Illusion," Pierce corrected. "I don't do tricks."

Ryan stopped. His eyes were steady on hers. "Illusion," she amended with a nod. "The specials would be broadcasted live, with a studio audience as well. The publicity—"

"You don't believe in magic, do you, Miss Swan?" There was the slightest of smiles on his mouth, the barest trace of amusement in his voice.

"Mr. Atkins, you're a very talented man," she said carefully. "I admire your work."

"A diplomat," he concluded, leaning back. "And a cynic. I like that."

Ryan didn't feel complimented. He was laughing at her without making the smallest attempt to conceal it. Your job, she reminded herself as her teeth clenched. Do your job. "Mr. Atkins, if we could discuss the terms of the contract—"

"I don't do business with anyone until I know who they are."

Ryan let out a quick breath. "My father—"

"I'm not talking to your father," Pierce interrupted smoothly.

"I didn't think to type up a bio," she snapped, then bit her tongue. Damn! She couldn't afford to lose her temper. But Pierce grinned, pleased.

"I don't think that will be necessary." He had her hand in his before she realized what he was doing.

"Nevermore."

The voice from behind had Ryan jolting in her chair.

"That's just Merlin," Pierce said mildly as she twisted her head.

There was a large black myna bird in a cage to her right. Ryan took a deep breath and tried to steady her nerves. The bird was staring at her.

"Very clever," she managed, eying the bird with some reservation. "Did you teach him to talk?"

"*Mmm.*"

"Buy you a drink, sweetie?"

Wide-eyed, Ryan gave a muffled laugh as she turned back to Pierce. He merely gave the bird a careless glance. "I haven't taught him manners."

She struggled not to be amused. "Mr. Atkins, if we could—"

"Your father wanted a son." Ryan forgot what she had been about to say and stared at him. "That made it difficult for you." Pierce was looking into her eyes again, her hand held loosely in his. "You're not married, you live alone. You're a realist who considers herself very practical. You find it difficult to control your temper, but you work at it. You're a very cautious woman, Miss Swan, slow to trust, careful in relationships. You're impatient because you have something to prove—to yourself and to your father."

His eyes lost their intense directness when he smiled at her. "A parlor game, Miss Swan, or telepathy?"

When Pierce released her hand, Ryan pulled it from the table into her lap. She hadn't cared for his accuracy.

"A little amateur psychology," he said comfortably, enjoying her stunned expression. "A basic knowledge of Bennett Swan and an understanding of body language." He shrugged his shoulders. "No trick, Miss Swan, just educated guesswork. How close was I?"

Ryan gripped her hands together in her lap. Her right palm was still warm from his. "I didn't come here to play games, Mr. Atkins."

"No." He smiled again, charmingly. "You came to close a deal, but I do things in my own time, in my own way. My profession encourages eccentricity, Miss Swan. Humor me."

"I'm doing my best," Ryan returned, then took a deep breath and sat back. "I think it's safe to say that we're both very serious about our professions."

"Agreed."

"Then you understand that it's my job to sign you with Swan, Mr. Atkins." Perhaps a bit of flattery would work, she decided. "We want you because you're the best in your field."

"I'm aware of that," he answered without batting an eye.

"Aware that we want you or that you're the best?" she found herself demanding.

He flashed her a very appealing grin. "Of both."

Ryan took a deep breath and reminded herself that entertainers were often impossible. "Mr. Atkins," she began.

With a flutter of wings, Merlin swooped out of his cage and landed on her shoulder. Ryan gasped and froze.

"Oh, God," she murmured. This was too much, she thought numbly. Entirely too much.

Pierce frowned at the bird as it settled its wings. "Odd, he's never done that with anyone before."

"Aren't I lucky," Ryan muttered, sitting perfectly still. Did birds bite? she wondered. She decided she didn't care to wait to find out. "Do you think you could—ah, persuade him to perch somewhere else?"

A slight gesture of Pierce's hand had Merlin leaving Ryan's shoulder to land on his own.

"Mr. Atkins, please, I realize a man in your profession would have a taste for—atmosphere." Ryan took a breath to steady herself, but it didn't work. "It's very difficult to discuss business in—in a dungeon," she said with a sweep of her arm. "With a crazed raven swooping down on me and . . ."

Pierce's shout of laughter cut her off. On his shoulder the bird settled his wings and stared, steely-eyed, at Ryan. "Ryan Swan, I'm going to like you. I work in this dungeon," he explained good-naturedly. "It's private and quiet. Illusions take more than skill; they take a great deal of planning and preparation."

"I understand that, Mr. Atkins, but—"

"We'll discuss business more conventionally over dinner," he interrupted.

Ryan rose as he did. She hadn't planned to stay more than an hour or two. It was a good thirty-minute drive down the cliff road to her hotel.

"You'll stay the night," Pierce added, as if he had indeed read her thoughts.

"I appreciate your hospitality, Mr. Atkins," she began, following as he walked back to the stairs, the bird remaining placidly on his shoulder. "But I have a reservation at a hotel in town. Tomorrow—"

"Do you have your bags?" Pierce stopped to take her arm before he mounted the steps.

"Yes, in the car, but—"

"Link will cancel your reservation, Miss Swan. We're in for a storm." He turned his head to glance at her. "I wouldn't like to think of you driving these roads tonight."

As if to accentuate his words, a blast of thunder greeted them as they came to the top of the stairs. Ryan murmured something. She wasn't certain she wanted to think of spending the night in this house.

"Nothing up my sleeve," Merlin announced.

She shot him a dubious look.

# Chapter Two

Dinner did much to put Ryan's mind at rest. The dining room was huge, with a roaring fire at one end and a collection of antique pewter at the other. The long refectory table was set with Sèvres china and Georgian silver.

"Link's an excellent cook," Pierce told her as the big man set a Cornish hen in front of her. Ryan caught a glimpse of his huge hands before Link left the room. Cautiously, she picked up her fork.

"He's certainly quiet."

Pierce smiled and poured a pale gold wine into her glass. "Link only talks when he has something to say. Tell me, Miss Swan, do you enjoy living in Los Angeles?"

Ryan looked over at him. His eyes were friendly now, not intense and intrusive, as they had been before. She allowed herself to relax. "Yes, I suppose I do. It's convenient for my work."

"Crowded?" Pierce cut into the poultry.

"Yes, of course, but I'm used to it."

"You've always lived in L.A.?"

"Except when I was in school."

Pierce noted the slight change in tone, the faintest hint of resentment no one else might have caught. He went on eating. "Where did you go to school?"

"Switzerland."

"A beautiful country." He reached for his wine. *And she didn't care to be shipped off,* he thought. "Then you began to work for Swan Productions?"

Frowning, Ryan stared into the fire. "When my father realized I was determined, he agreed."

"And you're a very determined woman," Pierce commented.

"Yes," she admitted. "For the first year, I shuffled papers, went for coffee, and was kept away from the talent." The frown vanished. A gleam of humor lit her eyes. "One day some papers came across my desk, quite by mistake. My father was trying to sign Mildred Chase for a miniseries. She wasn't cooperating. I did a little research and went to see her." Laughing with the memory, she sent Pierce a grin. "*That* was quite an experience. She lives in this fabulous place in the hills—guards, a dozen dogs. She's very 'old Hollywood.' I think she let me in out of curiosity."

"What did you think of her?" he asked, mainly to keep her talking, to keep her smiling.

"I thought she was wonderful. A genuine *grande dame.* If my knees hadn't been shaking, I'm sure I would have curtsied." A light of triumph covered her face. "And when I left two hours later, her signature was on the contract."

"How did your father react?"

"He was furious." Ryan picked up her wine. The fire sent a play of shadow and light over her skin. She was to think of the conversation later and wonder at her own expansiveness. "He raged at me for the better part of an hour." She drank, then set down the glass. "The next day, I had a promotion and a new office. Bennett Swan appreciates people who get things done."

"And do you," Pierce murmured, "get things done, Miss Swan?"

"Usually," she returned evenly. "I'm good at handling details."

"And people?"

Ryan hesitated. His eyes were direct again. "Most people."

He smiled, but his look remained direct. "How's your dinner?"

"My..." Ryan shook her head to break the gaze, then glanced down at her plate. She was surprised to see she had eaten a healthy portion of the hen. "It's very good. Your..." She looked back at him again, not certain what to call Link. *Servant? Slave?*

"Friend," Pierce put in mildly and sipped his wine.

Ryan struggled against the uncomfortable feeling that he saw inside her brain. "Your friend is a marvelous cook."

"Appearances are often deceiving," Pierce pointed out, amused. "We're both in professions that show an audience something that isn't real. Swan Productions deals in illusions. So do I." He reached toward her, and Ryan sat back quickly. In his hand was a long-stemmed red rose.

"Oh!" Surprised and pleased, Ryan took it from him. Its scent was strong and sweet. "I suppose that's the sort of thing you have to expect when you have dinner with a magician," she commented and smiled at him over the tip of the bud.

"Beautiful women and flowers belong together." The wariness that came into her eyes intrigued him. A very cautious woman, he thought again. He liked caution, respected it. He also enjoyed watching people react. "You're a beautiful woman, Ryan Swan."

"Thank you."

Her answer was close to prim and had his mouth twitching. "More wine?"

"No. No, thank you, I'm fine." But her pulse was throbbing lightly. Setting the flower beside her plate, she went back to her meal. "I've rarely been this far up the coast," she said conversationally. "Have you lived here long, Mr. Atkins?"

"A few years." He swirled the wine in his glass, but she noted he drank very little. "I don't like crowds," he told her.

"Except at a performance," she said with a smile.

"Naturally."

It occurred to Ryan, when Pierce rose and suggested they sit in the parlor, that they hadn't discussed the contract. She was going to have to steer him back to the subject.

"Mr. Atkins..." she began as they entered. "Oh! What a beautiful room!"

It was like stepping back to the eighteenth century. But there were no cobwebs, no signs of age. The furniture shone, and the flowers were fresh. A small upright piano stood in a corner with sheet music open. There were small, blown-glass figurines on the mantel. A menagerie, she noted on close study—unicorns, winged horses, centaurs, a three-headed hound. No conventional animals in Pierce Atkins's collection. Yet the fire in the grate was sedate, and the lamp standing on a piecrust table was certainly a Tiffany. It was a room Ryan would have expected to find in a cozy English country house.

"I'm glad you like it," Pierce said, standing beside her. "You seemed surprised."

"Yes. The outside looks like a prop from a 1945 horror movie, but..." Ryan stopped herself, horrified. "Oh, I'm sorry, I didn't mean..." But he was grinning, obviously delighted with her observation.

"It was used for just that more than once. That's why I bought it."

Ryan relaxed again as she wandered around the room. "It did occur to me that you might have chosen it for the atmosphere."

Pierce lifted a brow. "I have an—affection for things others take at face value." He stepped to a table where cups were already laid out. "I can't offer you coffee, I'm afraid. I don't use caffeine. The tea is herbal and very good." He was already pouring as Ryan stepped up to the piano.

"Tea's fine," she said absently. It wasn't printed sheet music on the piano, she noted, but staff paper. Automatically, she began to pick out the handwritten notes. The melody was hauntingly romantic. "This is beautiful." Ryan turned back to him. "Just beautiful. I didn't know you wrote music."

"I don't." Pierce set down the teapot. "Link does." He watched Ryan's eyes widen in astonishment. "Face value, Miss Swan?"

She lowered her eyes to her hands. "You make me quite ashamed."

"I've no intention of doing that." Crossing to her, Pierce took her hand again. "Most of us are drawn to beauty."

"But you're not?"

"I find surface beauty appealing, Miss Swan." Quickly, thoroughly, he scanned her face. "Then I look for more."

Something in the contact made her feel odd. Her voice wasn't as strong as it should have been. "And if you don't find it?"

"Then I discard it," he said simply. "Come, your tea will get cold."

"Mr. Atkins." Ryan allowed him to lead her to a chair. "I don't want to offend you. I can't afford to offend you, but . . ." She let out a frustrated breath as she sat. "I think you're a very strange man."

He smiled. She found it compelling, the way his eyes smiled a split second before his mouth. "You'd offend me, Miss Swan, if you didn't think so. I have no wish to be ordinary."

He was beginning to fascinate her. Ryan had always been careful to keep her professional objectivity when dealing with talent. It was important not to be awed. If you were awed, you'd find yourself adding clauses to contracts and making rash promises.

"Mr. Atkins, about our proposition."

"I've given it a great deal of thought." A crash of thunder shook the windows. Ryan glanced over as he lifted his cup. "The roads will be treacherous tonight." His eyes came back to Ryan's. Her hands had balled into fists at the blast. "Do storms upset you, Miss Swan?"

"No, not really." Carefully, she relaxed her fingers. "But I'm grateful for your hospitality. I don't like to drive in them." Lifting her cup, she tried to ignore the slashes of lightning. "If you have any questions about the terms, I'd be glad to go over them with you."

"I think it's clear enough." He sipped his tea. "My agent is anxious for me to accept the contract."

"Oh?" Ryan had to struggle to keep the triumph from her voice. It would be a mistake to push too soon.

"I never commit myself to anything until I'm certain it suits me. I'll tell you what I've decided tomorrow."

She nodded, accepting. He wasn't playing games, and she sensed that no agent, or anyone, would influence him beyond a certain point. He was his own man, first and last.

"Do you play chess, Miss Swan?"

"What?" Distracted, she looked up again. "I beg your pardon?"

"Do you play chess?" he repeated.

"Why, yes, I do."

"I thought so. You know when to move and when to wait. Would you like to play?"

"Yes," she agreed without hesitation. "I would."

Rising, he offered his hand and led her to a table by the windows. Outside, the rain hurled itself against the glass. But when she saw the chessboard already set up, she forgot the storm.

"They're exquisite!" Ryan lifted the white king. It was oversized and carved in marble. "Arthur," she said, then picked up the queen. "And Guinevere." She studied the other pieces. "Lancelot the knight, Merlin the bishop, and, of course, Camelot." She turned the castle over in her palm. "I've never seen anything like these."

"Take the white," he invited, seating himself behind the black. "Do you play to win, Miss Swan?"

She took the chair opposite him. "Yes, doesn't everyone?"

He gave her a long, unfathomable look. "No. Some play for the game."

After ten minutes Ryan no longer heard the rain on the windows. Pierce was a shrewd player and a silent one. She found herself watching his hands as they slid pieces over the board. They were long, narrow hands with nimble fingers. He wore a gold ring on his pinky with a scrolled symbol she didn't recognize. Ryan had heard it said those fingers could pick any lock, untie any knot. Watching them, she thought they were more suited for tuning a violin. When she glanced up, she found him watching her with his amused, knowing smile. She channeled her concentration on her strategy.

Ryan attacked, he defended. He advanced, she countered. Pierce was pleased to have a well-matched partner. She was a cautious player, given to occasional bursts of impulse. He felt her game-playing reflected who she was. She wouldn't be easily duped or easily beaten. He admired both the quick wits and the strength he sensed in her. It made her beauty all the more appealing.

Her hands were soft. As he captured her bishop, he wondered idly if her mouth would be, too, and how soon he would find out. He had already decided he would; now it was a matter of timing. Pierce understood the invaluable importance of timing.

"Checkmate," he said quietly and heard Ryan's gasp of surprise.

She studied the board a moment, then smiled over at him. "Damn, I didn't see that coming. Are you sure you don't have a few extra pieces tucked up your sleeve?"

"Nothing up my sleeve," Merlin cackled from across the room. Ryan shot him a glance and wondered when he had joined them.

"I don't use magic when skill will do," Pierce told her, ignoring his pet. "You play well, Miss Swan."

"You play better, Mr. Atkins."

"This time," he agreed. "You interest me."

"Oh?" She met his look levelly. "How?"

"In several ways." Sitting back, he ran a finger down the black queen. "You play to win, but you lose well. Is that always true?"

"No." She laughed but rose from the table. He was making her nervous again. "Do you lose well, Mr. Atkins?"

"I don't often lose."

When she looked back, he was standing at another table handling a pack of cards. Ryan hadn't heard him move. It made her uneasy.

"Do you know Tarot cards?"

"No. That is," she corrected, "I know they're for telling fortunes or something, aren't they?"

"Or something." He gave a small laugh and shuffled the cards gently. "Mumbo jumbo, Miss Swan. A device to keep someone's attention focused and to add mystery to quick thinking and observation. Most people prefer to be fooled. Explanations leave them disappointed. Even most realists."

"You don't believe in those cards." Ryan walked over to join him. "You know you can't tell the future with pasteboard and pretty colors."

"A tool, a diversion." Pierce lifted his shoulders. "A game, if you like. Games relax me." Pierce fanned the oversized cards in a quick, effective gesture, then spread them on the table.

"You do that very well," Ryan murmured. Her nerves were tight again, but she wasn't sure why.

"A basic skill," he said easily. "I could teach you quickly enough. You have competent hands." He lifted one, but it was her face he examined, not her palm. "Shall I pick a card?"

Ryan removed her hand. Her pulse was beginning to race. "It's your game."

With a fingertip, Pierce drew out a card and flipped it faceup. It was the Magician. "Confidence, creativity," Pierce murmured.

"You?" Ryan said flippantly to conceal the growing tension.

"So it might seem." Pierce laid a finger on another card and drew it out. The High Priestess. "Serenity," he said quietly. "Strength. You?"

Ryan shrugged. "Simple enough for you to draw whatever card you like after you've stacked the deck."

Pierce grinned, unoffended. "The cynic should choose the next to see where these two people will end. Pick a card, Miss Swan," he invited. "Any card."

Annoyed, Ryan plucked one and tossed it face up on the table. After a strangled gasp, she stared at it in absolute silence. The Lovers. Her heart hammered lightly at her throat.

"Fascinating," Pierce murmured. He wasn't smiling now, but he studied the card as if he'd never seen it before.

Ryan took a step back. "I don't like your game, Mr. Atkins."

"*Hmmm?*" He glanced up distractedly, then focused on her. "No? Well then…" He carelessly flipped the cards together and stacked them. "I'll show you to your room."

Pierce had been as surprised by the card as Ryan had been. But he knew reality was often stranger than any illusion he could devise. He had work to do, a great deal of final planning for his engagement in Las Vegas in two weeks time. Yet as he sat in his room, he was thinking of Ryan, not of the mechanics of his craft.

There was something about her when she laughed, something brilliant and vital. It appealed to him the same way her low-key, practical voice had appealed to him when she spoke of contracts and clauses.

He already knew the contract backward and forward. He wasn't a man to brush aside the business end of his profession. Pierce signed his name to nothing unless he understood every nuance. If the public saw him as mysterious, flashy and odd, that was all to the good. The image was part illusion, part reality. That was the way he preferred it. He had spent the second half of his life arranging things as he preferred them.

Ryan Swan. Pierce stripped off his shirt and tossed it aside. He wasn't certain about her just yet. He had fully intended to sign the contracts until he had seen her coming down the stairs. Instinct had made him hesitate. Pierce relied heavily on his instincts. Now he had some thinking to do.

The cards didn't influence him. He could make cards stand up and dance if that's what he wanted. But coincidence influenced him. It was odd that Ryan had turned over the card symbolizing lovers when he had been thinking what she would feel like in his arms.

With a laugh, he sat down and began to doodle on a pad of paper. The plans he was forming for a new escape would have to be torn up or revised, but it relaxed him to turn it over in his mind, just as he turned Ryan over in his mind.

It might be wise to sign her papers in the morning and send her on her way. He didn't care to have a woman intrude on his thoughts. But Pierce didn't always do what was wise. If he did, he would still be playing the club field, pulling rabbits out of his hat and colored scarves out of his pocket at union scale. Now he turned a woman into a panther and walked through a brick wall.

*Poof!* he thought. Instant magic. And no one remembered the years of frustration and struggle and failure. That, too, was exactly as he wanted it. There were few who knew where he had come from or who he had been before he was twenty-five.

Pierce tossed aside the pencil. Ryan Swan was making him uneasy. He would go downstairs and work until his mind was clear. It was then he heard her scream.

Ryan undressed carelessly. Temper always made her careless. Parlor tricks, she thought furiously and pulled down the zipper of her skirt. Show people. She should be used to their orchestrations by now.

She remembered a meeting with a well-known comedian the month before. He had tried out a twenty-minute routine on her before he had settled down to discuss plans for a guest appearance on a Swan Production presentation. All the business with the Tarot cards had been just a show, designed to impress her, she decided and kicked off her shoes. Just another ego trip for an insecure performer.

Ryan frowned as she unbuttoned her blouse. She couldn't agree with her own conclusions. Pierce Atkins didn't strike her as an insecure man—on stage or off. And she would have sworn he had been as surprised as she when she had turned over that card. Ryan shrugged out of her blouse and tossed it over a chair. Well, he was an actor, she reminded herself. What else was a magician but a clever actor with clever hands?

She remembered the look of his hands on the black marble chess pieces, their leanness, their grace. She shook off the memory. Tomorrow she would get his name on that contract and drive away. He had made her uneasy; even before the little production with the cards, he had made her uneasy. Those eyes, Ryan thought and shivered. There's something about his eyes.

It was simply that he had a very strong personality, she decided. He was magnetic and yes, very attractive. He'd cultivated that, just as he had no doubt cultivated the mysterious air and enigmatic smile.

Lightning flashed, and Ryan jolted. She hadn't been completely honest with Pierce: storms played havoc with her nerves. Intellectually, she could brush it aside, but lightning and thunder always had her stomach tightening. She hated the weakness, a primarily feminine weakness. Pierce had been right; Bennett Swan had wanted a son. Ryan had gone through her life working hard to make up for being born female.

Go to bed, she ordered herself. Go to bed, pull the covers over your head and shut your eyes. Purposefully, she walked over to draw the drapes. She stared at the window. Something stared back. She screamed.

Ryan was across the room like a shot. Her damp palms skidded off the knob. When Pierce opened the door, she fell into his arms and held on.

"Ryan, what the hell's going on?" He would have drawn her away, but the arms around his neck were locked tight. She was very small without her heels. He could feel the shape of her body as she pressed desperately against him. Through concern and curiosity, Pierce experienced a swift and powerful wave of desire. Annoyed, he pulled her firmly away and held her arms.

"What is it?" he demanded.

"The window," she managed, and would have been back in his arms again if he hadn't held her off. "At the window by the bed."

Setting her aside, he walked to it. Ryan put both hands to her mouth and backed into the door, slamming it.

She heard Pierce's low oath as he drew up the glass and reached outside. He pulled in a very large, very wet black cat. On a moan, Ryan slumped against the door.

"Oh, God, what next?" she wondered aloud.

"Circe." Pierce set the cat on the floor. She shook herself once, then leaped onto the bed. "I didn't realize she was outside in this." He turned to look at Ryan. If he had laughed at her, she would never have forgiven him. But there was apology in his eyes, not amusement. "I'm sorry. She must have given you quite a scare. Can I get you a brandy?"

"No." Ryan let out a long breath. "Brandy doesn't do anything for acute embarrassment."

"Being frightened is nothing to be embarrassed about."

Her legs were still shaking, so she stayed propped against the door. "You might warn me if you have any more pets." Making the effort, she managed a smile. "That way, if I wake up with a wolf in bed with me, I can shrug it off and go back to sleep."

He didn't answer. As she watched, his eyes drifted slowly down her body. Ryan became aware she wore only a thin silk teddy. She straightened bolt upright against the door. But when his eyes came back to hers, she couldn't move, couldn't speak. Her breath had started to tremble before he took the first step toward her.

*Tell him to go!* her mind shouted, but her lips wouldn't form the words. She couldn't look away from his eyes. When he stopped in front of her, her head tilted back so that the look continued to hold. She could feel her pulse hammer at her wrists, at her throat, at her breast. Her whole body vibrated with it.

*I want him.* The knowledge stunned her. *I've never wanted a man the way I want him.* Her breath was audible now. His was calm and even. Slowly, Pierce took his finger to her shoulder and pushed aside the strap. It fell loosely on her arm. Ryan didn't move. He watched her intensely as he brushed aside the second strap. The bodice of the teddy fluttered to the points of her breasts and clung tenuously. A careless movement of his hand would have it falling to her feet. She stood transfixed.

Pierce lifted both hands, pushing the hair back from her face. He let his fingers dive deep into it. He leaned closer, then hesitated. Ryan's lips trembled apart. He watched her eyes shut before his mouth touched hers.

His lips were firm and gentle. At first they barely touched hers, just tasted. Then he lingered for a moment, keeping the kiss soft. A promise or a threat; Ryan wasn't certain. Her legs were about to buckle. In defense, she curled her hands around his arms. There were muscles, hard, firm muscles that she wouldn't think of until much later. Now she thought only of his mouth. He was barely kissing her at all, yet the shock of the impact winded her.

Degree by aching degree he deepened the kiss. Ryan's fingers tightened desperately on his arms. His mouth brushed over hers, then came back with more pressure. His tongue feathered lightly over hers. He only touched her hair, though her body tempted him. He drew out every ounce of pleasure with his mouth alone.

He knew what it was to be hungry—for food, for love, for a woman—but he hadn't experienced this raw, painful need in years. He wanted the taste of her, only the taste of her. It was at once sweet and pungent. As he drew it inside him, he knew there would come a time when he would take more. But for now her lips were enough.

When he knew he had reached the border between backing away and taking her Pierce lifted his head. He waited for Ryan to open her eyes.

Her green eyes were darkened, cloudy. He saw that she was as stunned as she was aroused. He knew he could take her there, where they stood. He had only to kiss her again, had only to brush aside the brief swatch of silk she wore. But he did neither. Ryan's fingers loosened, then her hands dropped away from his arms. Saying nothing, Pierce moved around her and opened the door. The cat leaped off the bed to slip through the crack before Pierce shut it behind him.

# Chapter Three

By morning the only sign of the storm was the steady drip of water from the balcony outside Ryan's bedroom window. She dressed carefully. It was important that she be perfectly poised and collected when she went downstairs. It would have been easier if she could have convinced herself that she had been dreaming—that Pierce had never come to her room, that he had never given her that strange, draining kiss. But it had been no dream.

Ryan was too much a realist to pretend otherwise or to make excuses. A great deal of what had happened had been her fault, she admitted as she folded yesterday's suit. She had acted like a fool, screaming because a cat had wanted in out of the rain. She had thrown herself into Pierce's arms wearing little more than shattered nerves. And lastly and most disturbing she had made no protest. Ryan was forced to concede that Pierce had given her ample time to object. But she had done nothing, made no struggle, voiced no indignant protest.

Maybe he had hypnotized her, she thought grimly as she brushed her hair into order. The way he had looked at her, the way her mind had gone blank... With a sound of frustration, Ryan tossed the brush into her suitcase. You couldn't be hypnotized with a look.

If she was to deal with it, she first had to admit it. She had wanted him to kiss her. And when he had, her senses had ruled her. Ryan clicked the locks on the suitcase, then set it next to the door. She would have gone to bed with him. It was a cold, hard fact, and there was no getting around it. Had he stayed, she would have made love with him—a man she had known for a matter of hours.

Ryan drew a deep breath and gave herself a moment before opening the door. It was a difficult truth to face for a woman who prided herself on acting with common sense and practicality. She had come to get Pierce Atkins's name on a contract, not to sleep with him.

You haven't done either yet, she reminded herself with a grimace. And it was morning. Time to concentrate on the first and forget the second. Ryan opened the door and started downstairs.

The house was quiet. After peeking into the parlor and finding it empty, she continued down the hall. Though her mind was set on finding Pierce and completing the business she had come for, an open door to her right tempted her to stop. The first glance drew a sound of pleasure from her.

There were walls—literally walls—of books. Ryan had never seen so many in a private collection, not even her father's. Somehow she knew these books were more than an investment, they were read. Pierce would know each one of them. She walked into the room for a closer look. There was a scent of leather and of candles.

*The Unmasking of Robert Houdin,* by Houdini; *The Edge of the Unknown,* by Arthur Conan Doyle; *Les Illusionnistes et Leurs Secrets.* These and dozens of other books on magic and magicians Ryan expected.

But there was also T. H. White, Shakespeare, Chaucer, the poems of Byron and Shelley. Scattered among them were works by Fitzgerald, Mailer and Bradbury. Not all were leather bound or aged and valuable. Ryan thought of her father, who would know what each of his books cost, down to the last dollar and who had read no more than a dozen in his collection.

He has very eclectic taste, she mused as she wandered the room. On the mantelpiece were carved, painted figures she recognized as inhabitants of Tolkien's Middle Earth. There was a very modern metal sculpture on the desk.

Who is this man? Ryan wondered. Who is he really? Lyrical, fanciful, with hints of a firm realist beneath. It annoyed her to realize just how badly she wanted to discover the full man.

"Miss Swan?"

Ryan swung around to see Link filling the doorway. "Oh, good morning." She wasn't certain if his expression was disapproving or if it was simply her impression of his unfortunate face. "I'm sorry," she added. "Shouldn't I have come in here?"

Link lifted his massive shoulders in a shrug. "He would have locked it if he wanted you to stay out."

"Yes, of course," Ryan murmured, not certain if she should feel insulted or amused.

"Pierce said you can wait for him downstairs after you've had breakfast."

"Has he gone out?"

"Running," Link said shortly. "He runs five miles every day."

"Five miles?" But Link was already turning away. Ryan dashed across the room to keep up.

"I'll make your breakfast," he told her.

"Just coffee—tea," she corrected, remembering. She didn't know what to call him but realized that she would soon be too breathless from trying to keep pace with him to call him anything. "Link." Ryan touched his arm, and he stopped. "I saw your work on the piano last night." He was looking at her steadily, without any change of expression. "I hope you don't mind." He shrugged again. Ryan concluded he used the gesture often in place of words. "It's a beautiful melody," she continued. "Really lovely."

To her astonishment, he blushed. Ryan hadn't thought it possible for a man of his size to be embarrassed. "It's not finished," he mumbled, with his wide, ugly face growing pinker.

Ryan smiled at him, touched. "What is finished is beautiful. You have a wonderful gift."

He shuffled his feet, then mumbled something about getting her tea and lumbered off. Ryan smiled at his retreating back before she walked to the dining room.

Link brought her toast, with a grumble about her having to eat something. Ryan finished it off dutifully, thinking of Pierce's remark about face value. If nothing else came of her odd visit, she had learned something. Ryan didn't believe she would ever again make snap decisions about someone based on appearance.

Though she deliberately loitered over the meal, there was still no sign of Pierce when Ryan had finished. Reluctance to brave the lower floor again had her sipping at cold tea and waiting. At length, with a sigh, she rose, picked up her briefcase and headed down the stairs.

Someone had switched on the lights, and Ryan was grateful. The room wasn't brilliantly illuminated; it was too large for the light to reach all the corners. But the feeling of apprehension Ryan had experienced the day before didn't materialize. This time she knew what to expect.

Spotting Merlin standing in his cage, she walked over to him. The door of the cage was open, so she stood cautiously to the side as she studied him. She didn't want to encourage him to perch on her shoulder again, particularly since Pierce wasn't there to lure him away.

"Good morning," she said, curious as to whether he'd talk to her when she was alone.

Merlin eyed her a moment. "Buy you a drink, sweetie?"

Ryan laughed and decided Merlin's trainer had an odd sense of humor. "I don't fall for that line," she told him and bent down until they were eye to eye. "What else can you say?" she wondered out loud. "I bet he's taught you quite a bit. He'd have the patience for it." She grinned, amused that the bird seemed to be listening attentively to her conversation. "Are you a smart bird, Merlin?" she demanded.

"Alas, poor Yorick!" he said obligingly.

"Good grief, the bird quotes *Hamlet*." Shaking her head, Ryan turned toward the stage. There were two large trunks, a wicker hamper and a long, waist-high table. Curious, Ryan set down her briefcase and mounted the stairs. On the table was a deck of playing cards, a pair of empty cylinders, wine bottles and glasses and a pair of handcuffs.

Ryan picked up the playing cards and wondered fleetingly how he marked them. She could see nothing, even when she held them up to the light. Setting them aside, she examined the handcuffs. They appeared to be regulation police issue. Cold, steel, unsympathetic. She searched the table for a key and found none.

Ryan had done her research on Pierce thoroughly. She knew there wasn't supposed to be a lock made that could hold him. He had been shackled hand and foot and stuffed into a triple-locked steamer trunk. In less than three minutes he had been out, unmanacled. Impressive, she admitted, still studying the cuffs. Where was the trick?

"Miss Swan."

Ryan dropped the handcuffs with a clatter as she spun around. Pierce stood directly behind her. But he couldn't have come down the stairs, she thought. She would have heard, or certainly seen. Obviously, there was another entrance to his workroom. And how long, she wondered, had he been standing and watching? He was doing no more than that now while the cat busied herself by winding around his ankles.

"Mr. Atkins," she managed in a calm enough voice.

"I hope you slept well." He crossed to the table to join her. "The storm didn't keep you awake?"

"No."

For a man who had just run five miles, he looked remarkably fresh. Ryan remembered the muscles in his arms. There was strength in him, and obviously stamina. His eyes were very steady, almost measuring, on hers. There was no hint of the restrained passion she had felt from him the night before.

Abruptly, Pierce smiled at her, then gestured with his hand. "What do you see here?"

Ryan glanced at the table again. "Some of your tools."

"Ah, Miss Swan, your feet are always on the ground."

"I like to think so," she returned, annoyed. "What should I see?"

He seemed pleased with her response and poured a small amount of wine into a glass. "The imagination, Miss Swan, is an incredible gift. Do you agree?"

"Yes, of course." She watched his hands carefully. "To a point."

"To a point." He laughed a little and showed her the empty cylinders. "Can there be restrictions on the imagination?" He slipped one cylinder inside the other. "Don't you find the possibilities of the power of the mind over the laws of nature interesting?" Pierce placed the cylinders over the wine bottle, watching her.

Ryan was frowning at his hands now. "As a theory," she replied.

"But only a theory." Pierce slipped one cylinder out and set it over the wineglass. Lifting the first cylinder, he showed her that the bottle remained under it. "Not in practice."

"No." Ryan kept her eyes on his hands. He could hardly pull anything off right under her nose.

"Where's the glass, Miss Swan?"

"It's there." She pointed to the second cylinder.

"Is it?" Pierce lifted the tube. The bottle stood under it. With a sound of frustration, Ryan looked at the other tube. Pierce lifted it, revealing the partially filled glass. "They seem to have found the theory more viable," he stated and dropped the cylinders back in place.

"That's very clever," she said, irritated that she had stood inches away and not seen the trick.

"Would you care for some wine, Miss Swan?"

"No, I..."

Even as she spoke, Pierce lifted the cylinder. There, where she had just seen the bottle, stood the glass.

Charmed despite herself, Ryan laughed. "You're very good, Mr. Atkins."

"Thank you."

He said it so soberly, Ryan looked back at him. His eyes were calm and thoughtful. Intrigued, she tilted her head. "I don't suppose you'd tell me how you did it."

"No."

"I didn't think so." She lifted the handcuffs. The briefcase at the foot of the stage was, for the moment, forgotten. "Are these part of your act, too? They look real."

"They're quite real," he told her. He was smiling again, pleased that she had laughed. He knew it was a sound he would be able to hear clearly whenever he thought of her.

"There's no key," Ryan pointed out.

"I don't need one."

She passed the cuffs from hand to hand as she studied him. "You're very sure of yourself."

"Yes." The hint of amusement in the word made her wonder what twist his thoughts had taken. He held out his hands, wrists close. "Go ahead," he invited. "Put them on."

Ryan hesitated only a moment. She wanted to see him do it—right there in front of her eyes. "If you can't get them off," she said as she snapped the cuffs into place, "we'll just sit down and talk about those contracts." She glanced up at him, eyes dancing. "When you've signed them, we can send for a locksmith."

"I don't think we'll need one." Pierce held up the cuffs, dangling and open.

"Oh, but how..." She trailed off and shook her head. "No, that was too quick," she insisted, taking them back from him. Pierce appreciated the way her expression changed from astonishment to doubt. It was precisely what he had expected from her. "You had them made." She was turning them over, searching closely. "There must be a button or something."

"Why don't you try it?" he suggested and had the cuffs snapped on her wrists before she could decline. Pierce waited to see if she'd be angry. She laughed.

"I talked myself right into that one." Ryan gave him a good-humored grimace, then concentrated on the cuffs. She juggled her wrists. "They certainly feel real enough." Though she tried several different angles, the steel held firmly shut. "If there's a button," she muttered, "you'd have to dislocate your wrist to get to it." She tugged another moment, then tried to slip her hands through the opening. "All right, you win," she announced, giving up. "They're real." Ryan grinned up at him. "Can you get me out of these?"

"Maybe," he murmured, taking her wrists in his hands.

"That's a comforting answer," she returned dryly, but they both felt her pulse leap as his thumb brushed over it. He continued to stare down at her until she felt the same draining weakness she had experienced the night before. "I think," she began, her voice husky as she struggled to clear it. "I think you'd better..." The sentence trailed off as his fingers traced the vein in her wrist. "Don't," she said, not even certain what she was trying to refuse.

Silently, Pierce lifted her hands, slipping them over his head so that she was pressed against him.

She wouldn't allow it to happen twice. This time she would protest. "No." Ryan tugged once, uselessly, but his mouth was already on hers.

This time his mouth wasn't so patient or his hands so still. Pierce held her hips as his tongue urged her lips apart. Ryan fought against the helplessness—a helplessness that had more to do with her own needs than the restraints on her wrists. She was responding totally. Under the pressure of his, her lips were hungry. His were cool and firm while hers heated and softened. She heard him murmur something as he dragged her closer. An incantation, she thought dizzily. He was bewitching her; there was no other explanation.

But it was a moan of pleasure, not of protest, that slipped from her when his hands trailed up to the sides of her breasts. He drew slow, aching circles before his thumbs slipped between their bodies to stroke over her nipples. Ryan pressed closer, nipping at his bottom lip as she craved more. His hands were in her hair, pulling her head back so that his lips had complete command of hers.

Perhaps he was magic. His mouth was. No one else had ever made her ache and burn with only a kiss.

Ryan wanted to touch him, to make him hunger as desperately as she. She fretted against the restraints on her wrists, only to find her hands were free. Her fingers could caress his neck, run through his hair.

Then, as quickly as she had been captured, she was released. Pierce had his hands on her shoulders, holding her away.

Confused, still aching, Ryan stared up at him. "Why?"

Pierce didn't answer for a moment. Absently, he caressed her shoulders. "I wanted to kiss Miss Swan. Last night I kissed Ryan."

"You're being ridiculous." She started to jerk away, but his hands were suddenly firm.

"No. Miss Swan wears conservative suits and worries about contracts. Ryan wears silk and lace underneath and is frightened of storms. The combination fascinates me."

His words troubled her enough to make her voice cool and sharp. "I'm not here to fascinate you, Mr. Atkins."

"A side benefit, Miss Swan." He grinned, then kissed her fingers. Ryan jerked her hand away.

"It's time we settled our business one way or the other."

"You're right, Miss Swan." She didn't like the hint of amusement or the way he emphasized her name. Ryan found she no longer cared whether or not he signed the papers she carried. She simply wanted to shake loose of him.

"Well, then," she began and stooped to pick up her briefcase.

Pierce laid his hand over hers on the handle. His fingers closed gently. "I'm willing to sign your contracts with a few adjustments."

Ryan schooled herself to relax. Adjustments normally meant money. She'd negotiate with him and be done with it. "I'll be glad to discuss any changes you might want."

"That's fine. I'll want to work with you directly. I want you to handle Swan's end of the production."

"Me?" Ryan's fingers tightened on the handle again. "I don't get involved with the production end. My father—"

"I'm not going to work with your father, Miss Swan, or any other producer." His hand was still gently closed over hers, with the contracts between them. "I'm going to work with you."

"Mr. Atkins, I appreciate—"

"I'll need you in Vegas in two weeks."

"In Vegas? Why?"

"I want you to watch my performances—closely. There's nothing more valuable to an illusionist than a cynic. You'll keep me sharp." He smiled. "You're very critical. I like that."

Ryan heaved a sigh. She would have thought criticism would annoy, not attract. "Mr. Atkins, I'm a businesswoman, not a producer."

"You told me you were good at details," he reminded her amiably. "If I'm going to break my own rule and perform on television, I want someone like you handling the details. More to the point," he continued, "I want *you* handling the details."

"You're not being practical, Mr. Atkins. I'm sure your agent would agree. There are any number of people at Swan Productions who are better qualified to produce your special. I don't have any experience in that end of the business."

"Miss Swan, do you want me to sign your contracts?"

"Yes, of course, but—"

"Then make the changes," he said simply. "And be at Caesar's Palace in two weeks. I have a week run." Stooping, he lifted the cat into his arms. "I'll look forward to working with you."

# Chapter Four

When she stalked into her office at Swan Productions four hours later, Ryan was still fuming. He had nerve, she decided. She would give him top of the list for nerve. He thought he had her boxed into a corner. Did he really imagine he was the only name talent she could sign for Swan Productions? What outrageous conceit! Ryan slammed her briefcase down on her desk and flopped into the chair behind it. Pierce Atkins was in for a surprise.

Leaning back in her chair, Ryan folded her hands and waited until she was calm enough to think. Pierce didn't know Bennett Swan. Swan liked to run things his own way. Advice could be considered, discussed, but he would never be swayed on a major decision. As a matter of fact, she mused, he would more than likely go in the opposite direction he was pushed. He wouldn't appreciate being told who to put in charge of a production. Particularly, Ryan thought ruefully, when that person was his daughter.

There was going to be an explosion when she told her father of Pierce's conditions. Her only regret was that the magician wouldn't be there to feel the blast. Swan would find another hot property to sign, and Pierce could go back to making wine bottles disappear.

Ryan brooded into space. The last thing she wanted to do was worry about rehearsal calls and shooting schedules—and all the thousands of other niggling details involved in producing an hour show—not to mention the outright paranoia of it being a live telecast. What did she know about dealing with technical breakdowns and union rules and set designing? Producing was a complicated job. She had never had any desire to try her hand at that end of the business. She was perfectly content with the paperwork and preproduction details.

She leaned forward again, elbows on the desk, and cupped her chin in her hands. How foolish it is, she mused, to lie to yourself. And how fulfilling it would be to follow through on a project from beginning to end. She had ideas—so many ideas that were constantly being restricted by legal niceties.

Whenever she had tried to convince her father to give her a chance on the creative side, she had met the same unyielding wall. She didn't have the experience; she was too young. He conveniently forgot that she had been around the business all of her life and that she would be twenty-seven the following month.

One of the most talented directors in the business had done a film for Swan that had netted five Oscars. And he'd been twenty-six, Ryan remembered indignantly. How could Swan know if her ideas were gold or trash if he wouldn't listen to them? All she needed was one opportunity.

No, she had to admit that nothing would suit her better than to follow a project from signing to wrap party. But not this one. This time she would cheerfully admit failure and toss the contracts and Pierce Atkins right back in her father's lap. There was enough Swan in her to get her back up when given an ultimatum.

*Change the contracts.* With a snort of derision, Ryan flipped open her briefcase. He overplayed his hand, she thought, and now he'll... She stopped, staring down at the neatly stacked papers inside the case. On top of them was another long-stemmed rose.

"Now how did he..." Ryan's own laughter cut her off. Leaning back, she twirled the flower under her nose. He was clever, she mused, drawing in the scent. Very clever. But who the devil was he? What made him tick? Sitting there in her tailored, organized office, Ryan decided she very much wanted to know. Perhaps it would be worth an explosion and a bit of conniving to find out.

There were depths to a man who spoke quietly and could command with his eyes alone. Layers, she thought. How many layers would she have to peel off to get to the core of him? It would be risky, she decided, but... Shaking her head, Ryan reminded herself that she wasn't going to be given the opportunity to find out, in any case. Swan would either sign him on his own terms or forget him. She drew out the contracts, then snapped the briefcase shut. Pierce Atkins was her father's problem now. Still, she kept the rose in her hand.

The buzzer on her phone reminded her she didn't have time for daydreaming. "Yes, Barbara."

"The boss wants to see you."

Ryan grimaced at the intercom. Swan would have known she was back the moment she passed the guard at the gate. "Right away," she agreed. Leaving the rose on her desk, Ryan took the contracts with her.

Bennett Swan smoked an expensive Cuban cigar. He liked expensive things. More, he liked knowing his money could buy them. If there were two suits of equal cut and value, Swan would choose the one with the biggest price tag. It was a matter of pride.

The awards in his office were also a matter of pride. Swan Productions was Bennett Swan. Oscars and Emmys proved he was a success. The paintings and sculptures his art broker had advised him to purchase showed the world that he knew the value of success.

He loved his daughter, would have been shocked if anyone had said otherwise. There was no doubt in his mind that he was an excellent father. He had always given Ryan everything his money could buy: the best clothes, an Irish nanny when her mother had died, an expensive education, then a comfortable job when she had insisted on working.

He had been forced to admit that the girl had more on the ball than he had expected. Ryan had a sharp brain and a way of cutting through the nonsense and getting to the heart of a matter. It proved to him that the money spent on the Swiss school had been well spent. Not that he would begrudge his daughter the finest education. Swan expected results.

He watched the smoke curl from the tip of his cigar. Ryan had paid off for him. He was very fond of his daughter.

She knocked, then entered when he called out. He watched her cross the wide space of thick carpet to his desk. A pretty girl, he thought. Looks like her mother.

"You wanted to see me?" She waited for the signal to sit. Swan wasn't a big man but had always made up for his lack of size with expansiveness. The wide sweep of his arm told her to sit. His face was still handsome in the rugged, outdoorsy manner women found appealing. He had put on a bit of flesh in the last five years and had lost a bit of hair. Essentially, however, he looked the same as Ryan's earliest memory of him. Looking at him, she felt the familiar surge of love and frustration. Ryan knew too well the limitations of her father's affection for her.

"You're feeling better?" she asked, noting that his bout with the flu hadn't left any mark of sickness on him. His face was healthily ruddy, his eyes clear. With another sweeping gesture, he brushed the question aside. Swan was impatient with illness, particularly his own. He didn't have time for it.

"What did you think of Atkins?" he demanded the moment Ryan was settled. It was one of the small concessions Swan made to her, the asking of her opinion on another. As always, Ryan thought carefully before answering.

"He's a very unique man," she began in a tone that would have made Pierce smile. "He has extraordinary talent and a very strong personality. I'm not sure that one isn't the cause for the other."

"Eccentric?"

"No, not in the sense that he does things to promote an eccentric image." Ryan frowned as she thought of his house, his life-style. *Face value.* "I think he's a very deep man and one who lives precisely as he chooses. His profession is more than a career. He's dedicated to it the way an artist is to painting."

Swan nodded and blew out a cloud of expensive smoke. "He's hot box office."

Ryan smiled and shifted the contracts. "Yes, because he's probably the best at what he does, plus he's dynamic on stage and a bit mysterious off it. He seems to have locked up the beginnings of his life and tossed away the key. The public loves a puzzle. He gives them one."

"And the contracts?"

Here it comes, Ryan thought, bracing herself. "He's willing to sign, but with certain conditions. That is, he—"

"He told me about his conditions," Swan interrupted.

Ryan's carefully thought out dissertation was thrown to the winds. "He told you?"

"Phoned a couple of hours ago." Swan plucked the cigar from his mouth. The diamond on his finger shot light as he eyed his daughter. "He says you're cynical and dedicated to details. That's what he claims he wants."

"I simply don't believe his tricks were anything but clever staging," Ryan countered, annoyed that Pierce had spoken to Swan before she had. She felt, uncomfortably, as if she were playing chess again. He'd already outmatched her once. "He has a habit of incorporating his magic into the everyday. It's effective, but distracting at a business meeting."

"Insulting him seems to have turned the trick," Swan commented.

"I didn't insult him!" At that Ryan rose with the contracts in her hand. "I spent twenty-four hours in that house with talking birds and black cats, and I didn't insult him. I did everything I could to get his name on these except letting him saw me in half." She dropped the papers on her father's desk. "There are limits to what I'll do to humor the talent, no matter how hot they are at the box office."

Swan steepled his fingers and watched her. "He also said he didn't mind your temper. He doesn't like to be bored."

Ryan bit off the next words that sprang to mind. Carefully, she sat back down. "All right, you told me what he said to you. What did you say to him?"

Swan took his time answering. It was the first time anyone connected with the business had referred to Ryan's temper. Swan knew she had one and knew, too, that she kept it scrupulously controlled on the job. He decided to let it pass. "I told him we'd be glad to oblige him."

"You..." Ryan choked on the word and tried again. "You agreed? Why?"

"We want him. He wants you."

No explosion, she thought, not a little confused. What spell had Pierce used to manage this one? Whatever it was, she told herself grimly, she wasn't under it. She rose again. "Do I have any say in this?"

"Not as long as you work for me." Swan gave the contracts an idle glance. "You've been itching to do something along these lines for a couple of years," he reminded her. "I'm giving you your chance. And," he looked up then and met her eyes, "I'll be watching you closely. If you mess it up, I'll pull you."

"I'm not going to mess it up," she retorted, barely controlling a new wave of fury. "It'll be the best damn special Swan's ever produced."

"Just see that it is," he warned. "And that you don't go over budget. Take care of the changes and send the new contracts to his agent. I want him signed before the end of the week."

"He will be." Ryan scooped up the papers before she headed for the door.

"Atkins said you two would work well together," Swan added as she yanked the door open. "He said it was in the cards."

Ryan shot an infuriated glance over her shoulder before she marched out, slamming the door behind her.

Swan grinned a little. She certainly did favor her mother, he thought, then pushed a button to summon his secretary. He had another appointment.

If there was one thing Ryan detested, it was being manipulated. By the time her temper had cooled and she was back in her office, it dawned on her how smoothly both Pierce and her father had maneuvered her. She didn't mind it as much from Swan—he had had years to learn that to suggest she might not be able to handle something was the certain way to see that she did. Pierce was a different matter. He didn't know her at all, or shouldn't have. Yet he had handled her, subtly, expertly, in the same the-hand-is-quicker-than-the-eye fashion he had handled the empty cylinders. He had what he wanted. Ryan drafted out the new contracts and brooded.

She had gotten past that one little point, and she had what she wanted as well. She decided to look at the entire matter from a new angle. Swan Productions would have Pierce sewed up for three prime-time specials, and she would have her chance to produce.

*Ryan Swan, Executive Producer.* She smiled. Yes, she liked the sound of it. She said it again to herself and felt the first stirring of excitement. Pulling out her date book, Ryan began to calculate how quickly she could tie up loose ends and devote herself to the production.

Ryan had plowed through an hour's paper work when the phone interrupted her. "Ryan Swan," she answered briskly, balancing the receiver on her shoulder as she continued to scribble.

"Miss Swan, I've interrupted you."

No one else called her *Miss Swan* in just that way. Ryan broke off the sentence she had been composing and forgot it. "That's all right, Mr. Atkins. What can I do for you?"

He laughed, annoying her instantly.

"What's so funny?"

"You've a lovely business voice, Miss Swan," he said with the trace of humor still lingering. "I thought, with your penchant for detail, you'd like to have the dates I'll need you in Vegas."

"The contracts aren't signed yet, Mr. Atkins," Ryan began primly.

"I open on the fifteenth," he told her as if she hadn't spoken. "But rehearsals begin on the twelfth. I'd like you there for them as well." Ryan frowned, marking down the dates. She could almost see him sitting in his library, holding the cat in his lap. "I close on the twenty-first." She noted idly that the twenty-first was her birthday.

"All right. We could begin outlining the production of the special the following week."

"Good." Pierce paused a moment. "I wonder if I could ask you for something, Miss Swan."

"You could ask," Ryan said cautiously.

Pierce grinned and scratched Circe's ears. "I have an engagement in L.A. on the eleventh. Would you come with me?"

"The eleventh?" Ryan shifted the phone and turned back the pages of her desk calendar. "What time?"

"Two o'clock."

"Yes, all right." She marked it down. "Where should I meet you?"

"I'll pick you up—one-thirty."

"One-thirty. Mr. Atkins..." She hesitated, then picked up the rose on her desk. "Thank you for the flower."

"You're welcome, Ryan."

Pierce hung up, then sat for a moment, lost in thought. He imagined Ryan was holding the rose even now. Did she know that her skin was as soft as its petals? Her face, just at the jawline—he could still clearly feel its texture on his fingertips. He ran them down the cat's back. "What did you think of her, Link?"

The big man continued to push books back into place and didn't turn. "She has a nice laugh."

"Yes, I thought so, too." Pierce could remember the tone of it perfectly; it had been unexpected, a stark contrast to her serious expression of a moment before. Both her laugh and her passion had surprised him. He remembered the way her mouth had heated under his. He hadn't been able to work at all that night, thinking of her upstairs in bed with only that swatch of silk covering her.

He didn't like having his concentration disturbed, yet he was pulling her back. Instinct, he reminded himself. He was still following his instinct.

"She said she liked my music," Link murmured, still shuffling books.

Pierce glanced up, bringing his thoughts back. He knew how sensitive Link was about his music. "She did like it, very much. She thought the melody you'd left on the piano was beautiful."

Link nodded, knowing Pierce would tell him nothing but the truth. "You like her, don't you?"

"Yes." Pierce answered absently as he stroked the cat. "Yes, I believe I do."

"I guess you must want to do this TV thing."

"It's a challenge," Pierce replied.

Link turned then. "Pierce?"

*"Hmmm?"*

He hesitated to ask, afraid he already knew the answer. "Are you going to do the new escape in Las Vegas?"

"No." Pierce frowned, and Link felt a flood of relief. Pierce remembered that he'd been trying to work on that particular escape the night Ryan had stayed in his house in the room just down the hall from his own. "No, I haven't worked it all out yet." Link's relief was short-lived. "I'll use it for the special instead."

"I don't like it." It came out quickly, causing Pierce to look up again. "Too many things can go wrong."

"Nothing's going to go wrong, Link. It just needs some more work before I use it in the act."

"The timing's too close," Link insisted, taking an uncharacteristic step by arguing. "You could make some changes or just postpone it. I don't like it, Pierce," he said again, knowing it was useless.

"You worry too much," Pierce assured him. "It's going to be fine. I just have a few more things to work out."

But he wasn't thinking of the mechanics of his escape. He was thinking of Ryan.

# Chapter Five

Ryan caught herself watching the clock. *One-fifteen.* The days before the eleventh had gone quickly. She had been up to her ears in paper work, often working ten hours a day trying to clear her desk before the trip to Las Vegas. She wanted a clear road and no lingering contractual problems hanging over her head once she began work on the special. She would make up for lack of experience by giving the project all of her time and attention.

She still had something to prove—to herself, to her father, and now, to Pierce. There was more to Ryan Swan than contracts and clauses.

Yes, the days had gone quickly, she mused, but this last hour...*one-seventeen.* With a sound of annoyance, Ryan pulled out a file folder and opened it. She was watching the clock as if she were waiting for a date rather than a business appointment. That was ridiculous. Still, when the knock came, her head shot up and she forgot the neatly typed pages in the folder. Pushing away a surge of anticipation, Ryan answered calmly.

"Yes, come in."

"Hi, Ryan."

She struggled with disappointment as Ned Ross strolled into the room. He gave her a polished smile.

"Hello, Ned."

Ned Ross—thirty-two, blond and personable with casual California chic. He let his hair curl freely and wore expensive designer slacks with quiet silk shirts. No tie, Ryan noted. It went against his image, just as the subtle whiff of breezy cologne suited it. Ned knew the effects of his charm, which he used purposefully.

Ryan chided herself half-heartedly for being critical and returned his smile, though hers was a great deal cooler.

Ned was her father's second assistant. For several months, up to a few weeks ago, he had also been Ryan's constant escort. He had wined and dined her, given her a few thrilling lessons in surfing, showed her the beauty of the beach at sunset and made her believe she was the most attractive, desirable woman he had ever met. It had been a painful disillusionment when she had discovered he was more interested in cultivating Bennett Swan's daughter than Ryan herself.

"The boss wanted me to check in with you, see how things were shaping up before you take off for Vegas." He sat on the corner of her desk, then leaned over to give her a light kiss. He still had plans for his boss's daughter. "And I wanted to say good-bye."

"All my work's cleared up," Ryan told him, casually shifting the file folder between them. It was still difficult to believe that the attractive, tanned face and amiable smile masked an ambitious liar. "I intended to bring my father up to date myself."

"He's tied up," Ned told her easily and picked up the folder to flip through it. "Just took off for New York. Something on a location shoot he wants to see to personally. He won't be back until the end of the week."

"Oh." Ryan looked down at her hands. He might have taken a moment to call her, she thought, then sighed. When had he ever? And when would she ever stop expecting him to? "Well, you can tell him everything's taken care of." She took the folder back from him and set it down again. "I've a report written out."

"Always efficient." Ned smiled at her again but made no move to leave. He knew too well he had made a misstep with Ryan and had some lost ground to cover. "So, how do you feel about moving up to producer?"

"I'm looking forward to it."

"This Atkins," Ned continued, overlooking the coolness, "he's kind of a strange guy, isn't he?"

"I don't know him well enough to say," Ryan said evasively. She found she didn't want to discuss Pierce with Ned. The day she had spent with him was hers, personally. "I have an appointment in a few minutes, Ned," she continued, rising. "So if you'd—"

"Ryan." Ned took her hands in his as he had habitually done when they had dated. The gesture had always made her smile. "I've really missed you these past weeks."

"We've seen each other several times, Ned." Ryan allowed her hands to lie limply in his.

"Ryan, you know what I mean." He massaged her wrists gently but felt no increase in her pulse. His voice softened persuasively. "You're still angry with me for making that stupid suggestion."

"About using my influence with my father to have you head the O'Mara production?" Ryan lifted a brow. "No, Ned," she said evenly, "I'm not angry with you. I heard Bishop was given the job," she added, unable to resist the small jibe. "I hope you're not too disappointed."

"That's not important," he replied, masking his annoyance with a shrug. "Let me take you to dinner tonight." Ned drew her a fraction closer, and Ryan didn't resist. Just how far, she wondered, would he go? "That little French place you like so much. We could go for a drive up the coast and talk."

"Doesn't it occur to you that I might have a date?"

The question stopped him from lowering his mouth to hers. It hadn't occurred to him that she would be seeing anyone else. He was certain that she was still crazy about him. He had spent a lot of time and effort leading her to that end. He concluded she wanted to be persuaded.

"Break it," he murmured and kissed her softly, never noticing that her eyes stayed open and cold.

"No."

Ned hadn't expected a flat, unemotional refusal. He knew from experience that Ryan's emotions were easily tapped. He'd been prepared to disappoint a very friendly assistant director to be with Ryan again. Off guard, he raised his head to stare at her. "Come on, Ryan, don't be—"

"Excuse me." Ryan whipped her hands from Ned's and looked to the doorway. "Miss Swan," Pierce said with a nod.

"Mr. Atkins." She was flushed and furious to have been caught in a compromising situation in her own office. Why hadn't she told Ned to shut the door when he had come in? "Ned, this is Pierce Atkins. Ned Ross is my father's assistant."

"Mr. Ross." Pierce moved into the room but didn't extend his hand.

"A pleasure to meet you, Mr. Atkins." Ned flashed a smile. "I'm a big fan."

"Are you?" Pierce gave him a polite smile that made Ned feel as though he had been thrust into a very cold, very dark room.

His eyes faltered, then he turned back to Ryan. "Have a good time in Vegas, Ryan." He was already heading to the door. "Nice to have met you, Mr. Atkins."

Ryan watched Ned's hurried retreat with a frown. He had certainly lost his characteristic laid-back style. "What did you do to him?" she demanded when the door shut.

Pierce lifted a brow as he crossed to her. "What do you think I did?"

"I don't know," Ryan muttered. "But whatever you did to him don't ever do it to me."

"Your hands are cold, Ryan." He took them in his. "Why didn't you just tell him to go?"

He unnerved her when he called her Ryan. He unnerved her when he called her Miss Swan in the lightly mocking tone he used. Ryan looked down at their joined hands. "I did—that is, I was..." She caught herself, amazed that she was stammering out an explanation. "We'd better go if you're going to make your engagement, Mr. Atkins."

"Miss Swan." Pierce's eyes were full of humor as he lifted her hands to his lips. They were no longer cold. "I've missed that serious face and professional tone." Leaving her with nothing to say, Pierce took her arm and led her from the room.

Once they had settled in his car and joined the streaming traffic, Ryan tried for casual conversation. If they were going to be working closely together, she had to establish the correct relationship and quickly. *Queen's pawn to bishop two,* she thought, remembering the chess game. "What sort of engagement do you have this afternoon?"

Pierce stopped at a red light and glanced at her. His eyes met hers with brief but potent intensity. "A gig's a gig," he said enigmatically. "You're not fond of your father's assistant."

Ryan stiffened. He attacked, she defended. "He's good at his job."

"Why did you lie to him?" Pierce asked mildly when the light turned. "You could have told him you didn't want to have dinner with him instead of pretending you had a date."

"What makes you think I was pretending?" Ryan countered impulsively, hurt pride in her voice.

Pierce downshifted into second to take a corner and maneuvered his way around the point. "I simply wondered why you felt you had to."

Ryan didn't care for his calmness. "That's my affair, Mr. Atkins."

"Do you think we could drop the 'Mr. Atkins' for the afternoon?" Pierce pulled off into a lot and guided the car into a parking space. Then, turning his head, he smiled at her. He was, Ryan decided, entirely too charming when he smiled in just that way.

"Maybe," she agreed when her lips curved in response. "For the afternoon. Is Pierce your real name?"

"As far as I know." With this, he slid from the car. When Ryan climbed out her side, she noted they were in the parking lot of Los Angeles General Hospital.

"What are we doing here?"

"I have a show to do." Pierce took a black bag, not unlike one a doctor might use, from the trunk. "Tools of the trade," he told Ryan as she gave it a curious study. "No hypos or scalpels," he promised and held out a hand to her. His eyes were on hers, patient as she hesitated. Ryan accepted his hand, and together they walked through the side door.

Wherever Ryan had expected to spend the afternoon, it hadn't been in the pediatric ward of L.A. General. Whatever she had expected of Pierce Atkins, it hadn't been a communion with children. After the first five minutes, Ryan saw that he gave them much more than a show and a bagful of tricks. He gave himself.

Why, he's a beautiful man, she realized with something of a jolt. He plays in Vegas for thirty-five dollars a head, crams Covent Garden, but he comes here just to give a bunch of kids a good time. There were no reporters to note his humanitarianism and write it up in tomorrow's columns. He was giving his time and his talent for nothing more than bringing happiness. Or perhaps more accurately, she thought, relieving unhappiness.

That was the moment, though she didn't realize it, when Ryan fell in love.

She watched as he slipped a ball in and out of his fingers with continual motion. Ryan was as fascinated as the children. With a quick movement of his hand, the ball vanished, only to be plucked from the ear of a boy who squealed in delight.

His illusions were unsophisticated, flashy little bits of business an amateur could have performed. The ward was noisy with gasps and giggles and applause. It obviously meant more to Pierce than the thundering approval he heard on stage after a complicated feat of magic. His roots were there, among children. He had never forgotten it. He remembered too well the antiseptic and floral smell of a sick room and the confinement of a hospital bed. Boredom, he thought, could be the most debilitating disease there.

"You'll notice I brought along a beautiful assistant," Pierce pointed out. It took Ryan a moment to realize he meant her. Her eyes widened in astonishment, but he only smiled. "No magician travels without one, Ryan." He held out a hand, palm up. Amid giggles and applauses, she had no choice but to join him.

"What are you doing?" she demanded in a quick whisper.

"Making you a star," he said easily before turning back to the audience of children in beds and wheelchairs. "Ryan will tell you she keeps her lovely smile by drinking three glasses of milk every day. Isn't that so, Ryan?"

"Ah—yes." She glanced around at the expectant faces. "Yes, that's right." *What is he doing?* She'd never had so many large, curious eyes on her at one time.

"I'm sure everyone here knows how important it is to drink milk."

This was answered by some unenthusiastic agreements and a few muffled moans. Pierce looked surprised as he reached in his black bag and pulled out a glass already half-filled with white liquid. No one questioned why it hadn't spilled. "You do all drink milk, don't you?" He got laughter this time, along with more moans. Shaking his head, Pierce pulled out a newspaper and began to fashion it into a funnel. "This is a very tricky business. I don't know if I can make it work unless everyone promises to drink his milk tonight."

Immediately a chorus of promises sprang out. Ryan saw that he was as much Pied Piper as magician, as much psychologist as entertainer. Perhaps it was all the same. She noticed that Pierce was watching her with a lifted brow.

"Oh, I promise," she said agreeably and smiled. She was as entranced as the children.

"Let's see what happens," he suggested. "Do you suppose you could pour the milk from that glass into here?" he asked Ryan, handing her the glass. "Slowly," he warned, winking at the audience. "We wouldn't want to spill it. It's magic milk, you know. The only kind magicians drink." Pierce took her hand and guided it, holding the top of the funnel just above her eye level.

His palm was warm and firm. There hung about him some scent she couldn't place. It was of the outdoors, of the forest. Not pine, she decided, but something darker, deeper, closer to the earth. Her response to it was unexpected and unwanted. She tried to concentrate on holding the glass directly above the opening of the funnel. A few drops of milk dripped out of the bottom.

"Where do you buy magic milk?" one of the children wanted to know.

"Oh, you can't buy it," Pierce said gravely. "I have to get up very early and put a spell on a cow. There, now, that's good." Smoothly, Pierce dropped the empty glass back into his bag. "Now, if all's gone well..." He stopped, then frowned into the funnel. "This was my milk, Ryan," he said with a hint of censure. "You could have had yours later."

As she opened her mouth to speak, he whipped the funnel open. Automatically, she gasped and stepped back to keep from being splashed. But the funnel was empty.

The children shrieked in delight as she gasped at him. "She's still beautiful," he told the audience as he kissed Ryan's hand. "Even if she is greedy."

"I poured that milk myself," she stated later as they walked down the hospital corridor to the elevator. "It was dripping through the paper. I *saw* it."

Pierce nudged her into the elevator. "The way things seem and the way things are. Fascinating, isn't it, Ryan?"

She felt the elevator begin its descent and stood in silence for a moment. "You're not entirely what you seem, either, are you?"

"No. Who is?"

"You did more for those kids in an hour than a dozen doctors could have done." He looked down at her as she continued. "And I don't think it's the first time you've done this sort of thing."

"No."

"Why?"

"Hospitals are a hell of a place to be when you're a child," he said simply. It was all the answer he would give her.

"They didn't think so today."

Pierce took her hand in his again when they reached the first level. "There's no tougher audience than children. They're very literal-minded."

Ryan had to laugh. "I suppose you're right. What adult would have thought to ask you where you buy your magic milk?" She shot Pierce a look. "I thought you handled that one rather smoothly."

"I've had a bit of practice," he told her. "Kids keep you on your toes. Adults are more easily distracted by some clever patter and flash." He smiled down at her. "Even you. Though you watch me with very intriguing green eyes."

Ryan looked across the parking lot as they stepped outside. When he looked at her, it wasn't easy to focus on anything but him when he spoke. "Pierce, why did you ask me to come with you today?"

"I wanted your company."

Ryan turned back to him. "I don't think I understand."

"Do you have to?" he asked. In the sunlight her hair was the color of early wheat. Pierce ran his fingers through it, then framed her face with his hands as he had done that first night. "Always?"

Ryan's heart pounded in her throat. "Yes, I think..."

But his mouth was already on hers, and she could think no longer. It was just as it had been the first time. The gentle kiss drew everything from her. She felt a warm, fluttering ache pass through her as his fingers brushed her temple and then traveled to just under her heart. People walked by them, but she never knew. They were shadows, ghosts. The only things of substance were Pierce's mouth and hands.

Was it the wind she felt, or his fingers gliding over her skin? Did he murmur something, or had she?

Pierce drew her away. Ryan's eyes were clouded. They began to clear and focus as if she were coming out of a dream. He wasn't ready for the dream to end. Bringing her back, he took her lips again and tasted the dark, mysterious flavor of her.

He had to fight with the need to crush her against him, to savage her warm, willing mouth. She was a woman made for a gentle touch. Desire tore at him, and he suppressed it. There were times when he was locked in a dark, airless box that he had to push back the need to rush, the urge to claw his way out. Now he almost felt the same hint of panic. *What was she doing to him?* The question ran through his mind even as he brought her closer. Pierce knew only that he wanted her with a desperation he hadn't thought himself capable of.

Was there silk next to her skin again? Thin, fragile silk lightly scented with the fragrance she wore? He wanted to make love to her by candlelight or in a field with the sun pouring over her. Dear God, how he wanted her.

"Ryan, I want to be with you." The words were whispered inside her mouth and made her tremble. "I need to be with you. Come with me now." With his hands he tilted her head to another angle and kissed her again. "Now, Ryan. Let me love you."

"Pierce." She was sinking and struggling to find solid ground. She leaned against him even as she shook her head. "I don't know you."

Pierce controlled a sudden wild desire to drag her to his car, to take her back to his home. To his bed. "No." He said it as much to himself as to Ryan. Drawing her away, he held her by the shoulders and studied her. "No, you don't. And Miss Swan would need to." He didn't like the erratic beating of his heart. Calm and control were intimate parts of his work, and therefore, of him. "When you know me," he told her quietly, "we'll be lovers."

"No." Ryan's objection sprang from his matter-of-fact tone, not from the statement. "No, Pierce, we won't be lovers unless it's what I want. I make deals on contracts, not in my personal life."

Pierce smiled, more relaxed with her annoyance than he would have been with malleability. Anything that came too easily he suspected. "Miss Swan," he murmured as he took her arm. "We've already seen the cards."

# Chapter Six

Ryan arrived in Las Vegas alone. She had insisted on it. Once her nerves had settled and she had been able to think practically, she had decided it would be unwise to have too much personal contact with Pierce. When a man was able to make you forget the world around you with a kiss, you kept your distance. That was Ryan Swan's new rule.

Through most of her life she had been totally dominated by her father. She had been able to do nothing without his approval. He might not have given her his time, but he had always given her his opinion. And his opinion had been law.

It was only upon reaching her early twenties that Ryan had begun to explore her own talents, her own independence. The taste of freedom had been very sweet. She wasn't about to allow herself to be dominated again, certainly not by physical needs. She knew from experience that men weren't particularly trustworthy. Why should Pierce Atkins be any different?

After paying off the cab, Ryan took a moment to look around. It was her first trip to Vegas. Even at ten in the morning it was an eye-opener. The Strip stretched long in both directions, and lining it were names like The Dunes, The Sahara, The MGM. The hotels vied for attention with gushing fountains, elaborate neon and fabulous flowers.

Billboards announced famous names in huge letters. Stars, stars, stars! The most beautiful women in the world, the most talented performers, the most colorful, the most exotic—they were all here. Everything was packed together; an adult amusement park circled by desert and ringed by mountains. The morning sun baked the streets; at night the neon would light them.

Ryan turned and looked at Caesar's Palace. It was huge and white and opulent. Above her head in enormous letters was Pierce's name and the dates of his engagements. What sort of feeling did it give a man like him, she wondered, to see his name advertised so boldly?

She lifted her bags and took the moving walkway that would transport her past the glittering fountain and Italian statues. In the morning quiet she could hear the water spurt up and splash down. She imagined that at night the streets would be noisy, filled with cars and people.

The moment she entered the hotel lobby, Ryan heard the whirl and chink of the slot machines. She had to curb a desire to walk into the casino for a look instead of going to the front desk.

"Ryan Swan." She set down her suitcases at the foot of the long counter. "I have a reservation."

"Yes, Miss Swan." The desk clerk beamed at her without checking his files. "The bellboy will take your bags." He signaled, then handed a key to the answering bellboy. "Enjoy your stay, Miss Swan. Please let us know if there's anything we can do for you."

"Thank you." Ryan accepted the clerk's deference without a thought. When people knew she was Bennett Swan's daughter, they treated her like a visiting dignitary. It was nothing new and only mildly annoy-ing.

The elevator took her all the way to the top floor with the bellboy keeping a respectful silence. He led the way down the corridor, unlocked the door, then stepped back to let her enter.

Ryan's first surprise was that it wasn't a room but a suite. Her second was that it was already occupied. Pierce sat on the sofa working with papers he had spread out on the table in front of him.

"Ryan." He rose, then, going to the bellboy, handed him a bill. "Thank you."

"Thank *you*, Mr. Atkins."

Ryan waited until the door shut behind him. "What are you doing here?" she demanded.

"I have a rehearsal scheduled this afternoon," he reminded her. "How was your flight?"

"It was fine," she told him, annoyed with his an-swer and with the suspicions that were creeping into her mind.

"Can I get you a drink?"

"No, thank you." She glanced around the well-appointed room, took a brief glimpse out the window, then gestured broadly. "What the hell is this?"

Pierce lifted a brow at her tone but answered mildly. "Our suite."

"Oh, no," she said with a definite shake of her head. "*Your* suite." Picking up her bags, she headed for the door.

"Ryan." It was the calm quality of his voice that stopped her—and that snapped her temper.

"What a very small, very dirty trick!" Ryan dropped her bags with a thud and turned on him. "Did you really think you could change my reservation and—and—"

"And what?" he prompted.

She gestured around the room again. "Set me up here with you without me making a murmur? Did you really think I'd pop cozily into your bed because you arranged it so nicely? How *dare* you! How dare you lie to me about needing me to watch you perform when all you wanted was for me to keep your bed warm!"

Her voice had changed from low accusation to high fury before Pierce grabbed her wrist. The strength in his fingers had her gasping in surprise and alarm. "I don't lie," Pierce said softly, but his eyes were darker than she had ever seen them. "And I don't need tricks to find a woman for my bed."

She didn't try to free herself. Instinct warned her against it, but she couldn't control her temper. "Then what do you call this?" she tossed back.

"A convenient arrangement." He felt her pulse racing under his fingers. Anger made his voice dangerously cool.

"For whom?" she demanded.

"We'll need to talk over a number of things in the next few days." He spoke with quiet deliberation, but his grip never slackened. "I don't intend to run down to your room every time I have something to say to you. I'm here to work," he reminded her. "And so are you."

"You should have consulted me."

"I didn't," he countered icily. "And I don't sleep with a woman unless she wants me to, Miss Swan."

"I don't appreciate you taking it upon yourself to change arrangements without discussing it with me first." Ryan stood firm on this, though her knees were threatening to tremble. His fury was all the more frightening in its restraint.

"I warned you before, I do things in my own way. If you're nervous, lock your door."

The jibe made her voice sharp. "A lot of good that would do with you. A lock would hardly keep you out."

His fingers tightened on her wrist quickly, painfully, before he tossed it aside. "Perhaps not." Pierce opened the door. "But a simple *no* would."

He was gone before Ryan could say any more. She leaned back against the door as the shudders ran through her. Until that moment she hadn't realized how badly she had been frightened. She was accustomed to dealing with histrionic bursts of temper or sulky silences from her father. But this . . .

There had been ice-cold violence in Pierce's eyes. Ryan would rather have faced the raging, shouting fury of any man than the look that could freeze her.

Without knowing she did so, Ryan rubbed her wrist. It throbbed lightly in each separate spot that Pierce's fingers had gripped. She had been right when she had said she didn't know him. There was more to him than she had ever guessed. Having uncovered one layer, she wasn't entirely certain she could deal with what she had discovered. For another moment she leaned against the door, waiting for the shaking to stop.

She looked around the room. Perhaps she had been wrong to have reacted so strongly to a harmless business arrangement, she finally decided. Sharing a suite was essentially the same thing as having adjoining rooms. If that had been the case, she would have thought nothing of it.

But he had been wrong, too, she reminded herself. They might have come to an easy agreement about the suite if he had only discussed it with her first. She had promised herself when she had left Switzerland that she would no longer be directed.

And Pierce's phrasing had worried her. *He didn't sleep with a woman unless she wanted him to.* Ryan was too aware that they both knew she wanted him.

A simple *no* would keep him out. Yes, she mused as she picked up her bags. That she could depend on. He would never force himself on any woman—very simply, he would have no need to. She wondered how long it would be before she forgot to say no.

Ryan shook her head. The project was as important to Pierce as it was to her. It wasn't smart to start off by bickering over sleeping arrangements or worrying about remote possibilities. She knew her own mind. She went to unpack.

When Ryan went down to the theatre, the rehearsal was already underway. Pierce held center stage. There was a woman with him. Even though she was dressed plainly in jeans and a bulky sweatshirt, Ryan recognized the statuesque redhead who was Pierce's assistant. On the tapes, Ryan recalled, she had worn brief, sparkling costumes or floaty dresses. *No magician travels without a beautiful assistant.*

Hold on, Ryan, she warned herself. No business of yours. Quietly, she walked down and took a seat in the center of the audience. Pierce never glanced in her direction. Hardly aware of what she did, Ryan began to think of camera angles and sets.

Five cameras, she thought, and nothing too showy in the background. Nothing glittery to pull attention away from him. Something dark, she decided. Something to enhance the image of wizard or warlock rather than showman.

It came as a complete surprise to her when Pierce's assistant drifted slowly backward until she was lying horizontally in thin air. Ryan stopped planning and watched. He used no patter now but only gestures—wide, sweeping gestures that brought black capes and candlelight to mind. The woman began revolving, slowly at first and then with greater speed.

Ryan had seen the illusion on tape, but seeing it in the flesh was a totally different experience. There were no props to distract from the two at stage center, no costumes, music or flashing lights to enhance the mood. Ryan discovered she was holding her breath and forced herself to let it out. The woman's cap of red curls fluttered as she spun. Her eyes were closed, her face utterly peaceful while her hands were folded neatly at her waist. Ryan watched closely, looking for wires, for gimmicks. Frustrated, she leaned forward.

She couldn't prevent a small gasp of appreciation as the woman began to roll over and over as she continued to spin. The calm expression on her face remained unchanged, as if she slept rather than whirled and circled three feet above the stage floor. With a gesture, Pierce stopped the motion, bringing her vertical again, slowly, until her feet touched the stage. When he passed his hand in front of her face, she opened her eyes and grinned.

"How was it?"

Ryan almost jolted at the commonplace words that bounced cheerfully off the theater walls.

"Good," Pierce said simply. "It'll be better with the music. I want red lights, something hot. Start soft and then build with the speed." He gave these orders to the lighting director before turning back to his assistant. "We'll work on the transportation."

For an hour Ryan watched, fascinated, frustrated and undeniably entertained. What seemed to her flawless, Pierce repeated again and again. With each illusion, he had his own ideas of the technical effects he wanted. Ryan could see that his creativity didn't stop at magic. He knew how to use lighting and sound to enhance, accent, underline.

A perfectionist, Ryan noted. He worked quietly, without the dynamics he exuded in a performance. Nor was there the careless ease about him she had seen when he had entertained the children. He was working. It was a plain and simple fact. A wizard, perhaps, she mused with a smile, but one who pays his dues with long hours and repetition. The longer she watched, the more respect she felt.

Ryan had wondered what it would be like to work with him. Now she saw. He was relentless, tireless and as fanatical about details as she was herself. They were going to argue, she predicted and began to look forward to it. It was going to be one hell of a show.

"Ryan, would you come up, please?"

She was startled when he called her. Ryan would have sworn he hadn't known she was in the theater. Fatalistically, she rose. It was beginning to appear that there was nothing he didn't know. As Ryan came forward, Pierce said something to his assistant. She gave a quick, lusty laugh and kissed him on the cheek.

"At least I get to stay all in one piece on this run," she told him, then turned to grin at Ryan as she mounted the stage.

"Ryan Swan," Pierce said, "Bess Frye."

On closer study Ryan saw the woman wasn't a beauty. Her features were too large for classic beauty. Her hair was brilliantly red and cropped into curls around a large-boned face. Her eyes were almost round and shades darker than Ryan's green. Her make-up was as exotic as her clothes were casual, and she was nearly as tall as Pierce.

"Hi!" There was a burst of friendliness in the one word. Bess extended her hand to give Ryan's an enthusiastic shake. It was hard to believe that the woman, as solid as a redwood, had been spinning three feet above the stage. "Pierce has told me all about you."

"Oh?" Ryan glanced over at him.

"Oh, yeah." She rested an elbow on his shoulder as she spoke to Ryan. "Pierce thinks you're real smart. He likes the brainy type, but he didn't say you were so pretty. How come you didn't tell me she was so pretty, sweetie?" It didn't take Ryan long to discover that Bess habitually spoke in long, explosive bursts.

"And have you accuse me of seeing a woman only as a stage prop?" He dipped his hands into his pockets.

Bess gave another burst of lusty laughter. "He's smart, too," she confided to Ryan, giving Pierce a squeeze. "You're going to be the producer on this special?"

"Yes." A little dazed by the overflowing friendliness, Ryan smiled. "Yes, I am."

"Good. About time we had a woman running things. I'm surrounded by men in this job, sweetie. Only one woman in the road crew. We'll have a drink sometime soon and get acquainted."

*Buy you a drink, sweetie?* Ryan remembered. Her smile became a grin. "I'd like that."

"Well, I'm going to see what Link's up to before the boss decides to put me back to work. See you later." Bess strode off stage—six feet of towering enthusiasm. Ryan watched her all the way.

"She's wonderful," Ryan murmured.

"I've always thought so."

"She seems so cool and reserved on stage." Ryan smiled up at Pierce. "Has she been with you long?"

"Yes."

The warmth Bess had brought was rapidly fading. Clearing her throat, Ryan began again. "The rehearsal went very well. We'll have to discuss which illusions you plan to incorporate into the special and whatever new ones you intend to develop."

"All right."

"There'll have to be some adjustments, naturally, for television," she continued, trying to overlook his monosyllabic responses. "But basically I imagine you want a condensed version of your club act."

"That's right."

In the short time Ryan had known Pierce, she had come to learn he possessed a natural friendliness and humor. Now he was looking at her with his eyes guarded, obviously impatient for her to leave. The apology she had planned couldn't be made to this man.

"I'm sure you're busy," she said stiffly and turned away. It hurt, she discovered, to be shut out. He had no right to hurt her. Ryan left the stage without looking back.

Pierce watched her until the doors at the back of the theatre swung shut behind her. With his eyes still on the door, he crushed the ball he held in his hand until it was flat. He had very strong fingers, strong enough to have snapped the bones of her wrist instead of merely bruising it.

He hadn't liked seeing those bruises. He didn't like remembering how she had accused him of trying to take her by deceit. He had never had to take any woman by deceit. Ryan Swan would be no different.

He could have had her that first night with the storm raging outside and her body pressed close to his.

*And why didn't I?* he demanded of himself and tossed the mangled ball aside. Why hadn't he taken her to bed and done all the things he had so desperately wanted to do? Because she had looked up at him with her eyes full of panic and acceptance. She had been vulnerable. He had realized, with something like fear, that he had been vulnerable, too. And still she haunted his mind.

When she had walked into the suite that morning, Pierce had forgotten the careful notes he had been making on a new illusion. He had seen her, walking in wearing one of those damn tailored suits, and he had forgotten everything. Her hair had been windblown from the drive, like the first time he had seen her. And all he had wanted to do was hold her—to feel the small, soft body yield against his.

Perhaps his anger had started to grow even then, to fire up with her words and accusing eyes.

He shouldn't have hurt her. Pierce stared down at his empty hands and swore. He had no right to mark her skin—the ugliest thing a man could do to a woman. She was weaker than he, and he had used that—used his temper and his strength, two things he had promised himself long, long ago he would never use on a woman. In his mind no provocation could justify it. He could blame no one but himself for the lapse.

He couldn't dwell on it or on Ryan any longer and continue to work. He needed his concentration. The only thing to do was to put their relationship back where Ryan had wanted it from the beginning. They would work together successfully, and that would be all. He had learned to control his body through his mind. He could control his needs, his emotions, the same way.

With a final oath Pierce walked back to talk with his road crew about props.

# Chapter Seven

Las Vegas was difficult to resist. Inside the casinos it was neither day nor night. Without clocks and with the continual clinking of slots, there was a perpetual time-lessness, an intriguing disorientation. Ryan saw people in evening dress continuing a night's gambling into late morning. She watched thousands of dollars change hands at the blackjack and baccarat tables. More than once she held her breath while the roulette wheel spun with a small fortune resting on the caprices of the silver ball.

She learned that the fever came in many forms—cool, dispassionate, desperate, intense. There was the woman feeding the nickel slot machine and the dedicated player tossing the dice. Smoke hung in the air over the sounds of winning and of losing. The faces would change, but the mood remained. Just one more roll of the dice, one more pull of the lever.

The years in the prim Swiss school had cooled the gambling blood Ryan had inherited from her father. Now, for the first time, Ryan felt the excitement of the urge to test Lady Luck. She refused it, telling herself she was content to watch. There was little else for her to do.

She saw Pierce onstage at rehearsals and hardly at all otherwise. It was amazing to her that two people could share a suite and so rarely come into contact with each other. No matter how early she rose, he was already gone. Once or twice after she was long in bed, Ryan heard the quick click of the lock on the front door. When they spoke, it was only to discuss ideas on how to alter his club act for television. Their conversations were calm and technical.

He's trying to avoid me, she thought the night of his opening performance, and doing a damn good job of it. If he had wanted to prove that sharing a suite meant nothing personal, he had succeeded beautifully. That, of course, was what she wanted, but she missed the easy camaraderie. She missed seeing him smile at her.

Ryan decided to watch the show from the wings. There she would have a perfect view and be in a position to note Pierce's timing and style while getting a backstage perspective. Rehearsals had given her an insight into his work habits, and now she would watch him perform from as close to his point of view as she could manage. She wanted to see more than the audience or a camera would see.

Careful to stay out of the way of the stagehands and grips, Ryan settled herself into a corner and watched. From the first wave of applause as he was introduced, Pierce had his audience in the palm of his hand. *My God, he's beautiful!* she thought as she studied his style and flare. Dynamic, dramatic, his personality alone would have held the audience. The charisma he possessed was no illusion but as integral a part of him as the color of his hair. He dressed in black, as was his habit, needing no brilliant colors to keep eyes glued to him.

He spoke as he performed. Patter, he would have called it, but it was much more. He tuned the mood with words and cadence. He could string them along, then dazzle them completely—a shot of flame from his naked palm, a glittering silver pendulum that swung, unsupported, in thin air. He was no longer pragmatic, as he had been in rehearsals, but dark and mysterious.

Ryan watched as he was padlocked into a duffel bag, slipped into a chest and chained inside. Standing on it, Bess pulled up a curtain and counted to twenty. When the curtain dropped, Pierce himself stood on the chest in a complete costume change. And, of course, when he unlocked the chest and bag, Bess was inside. He called it transportation. Ryan called it incredible.

His escapes made her uneasy. Watching volunteers from the audience nail him into a sturdy packing crate she herself had examined had her palms dampening. She could imagine him in the dark, airless box and feel her own breath clogging in her lungs. But his freedom was accomplished in less than two minutes.

For the finale, he locked Bess in a cage, curtaining it and levitating it to the ceiling. When he brought it down moments later, there was a sleek young panther in her place. Watching him, seeing the intensity of his eyes, the mysterious hollows and shadows on his face, Ryan almost believed he had transcended the laws of nature. For that moment before the curtain came down, the panther was Bess and he was more enchanter than showman.

Ryan wanted to ask him, convince him to explain just this one illusion in terms she could understand. When he came offstage and their eyes held, she swallowed the words.

His face was damp from the lights and his own concentration. She wanted to touch him, finding, to her own astonishment, that watching him perform had aroused her. The drive was more basic and more powerful than anything she had ever experienced. She could imagine him taking her with his strong, clever hands. Then his mouth, his impossibly sensual mouth, would be on hers, taking her to that strange, weightless world he knew. If she went to him now—offered, demanded—would she find him as hungry as herself? Would he say nothing, only lead her away to show her his magic?

Pierce stopped in front of her, and Ryan stepped back, shaken by her own thoughts. Her blood was heated, churning under her skin, demanding that she make the move toward him. Aware, aroused but unwilling, she kept her distance.

"You were marvelous," she said but heard the stiffness in the compliment.

"Thank you." Pierce said nothing more as he moved past her.

Ryan felt pain in her palms and discovered she was digging her nails into her flesh. This has got to stop, she told herself and turned to go after him.

"Hey, Ryan!" She stopped as Bess poked her head out of her dressing room. "What did you think of the show?"

"It was wonderful." She glanced down the corridor; Pierce was already out of reach. Perhaps it was for the best. "I don't suppose you'd let me in on the secret of the finale?" she asked.

Bess laughed. "Not if I value my life, sweetie. Come on in, talk to me while I change."

Ryan obliged, closing the door behind her. The air tingled with the scents of greasepaint and powder. "It must be quite an experience, being turned into a panther."

"Oh, lord, Pierce has turned me into everything imaginable that walks, crawls or flies; he's sawed me to pieces and balanced me on swords. In one gag he had me sleeping on a bed of nails ten feet above the stage." As she spoke, she stripped out of her costume with no more modesty than a five-year-old.

"You must trust him," Ryan commented as she looked around for an empty chair. Bess had a habit of strewing her things over all available space.

"Just toss something out of your way," she suggested as she plucked a peacock blue robe from the arm of a chair. "Trust Pierce?" she continued as she belted the robe. "He's the best." Sitting at the vanity, she began to cream off her stage make-up. "You saw how he is at rehearsals."

"Yes." Ryan folded a crumpled blouse and set it aside. "Exacting."

"That's not the half of it. He works out his illusions on paper, then goes over them again and again in that dungeon of his before he even thinks about showing anything to me or Link." She looked at Ryan with one eye heavily mascaraed and the other naked. "Most people don't know how hard he works because he makes it look so easy. That's the way he wants it."

"His escapes," Ryan began as she straightened Bess's clothes. "Are they dangerous?"

"I don't like some of them." Bess tissued off the last of the cream. Her exotic face was unexpectedly young and fresh. "Getting out of manacles and a straight-jacket are one thing." She shrugged as she rose. "But I've never liked it when he does his version of Houdini's Water Torture or his own A Thousand Locks."

"Why does he do it, Bess?" Ryan set a pair of jeans aside but continued to roam the room restlessly. "His illusions would be enough."

"Not for Pierce." Bess dropped the robe, then snapped on a bra. "The escapes and the danger are important to him. They always have been."

"Why?"

"Because he wants to test himself all the time. He's never satisfied with what he did yesterday."

"Test himself," Ryan murmured. She had sensed this herself but was a long way from understanding it. "Bess, how long have you been with him?"

"Since the beginning," Bess told her as she tugged on jeans. "Right from the beginning."

"Who is he?" Ryan demanded before she could stop herself. "Who is he really?"

With a shirt hanging from her fingertips, Bess gave Ryan a sudden, penetrating glance. "Why do you want to know?"

"He..." Ryan stopped, not knowing what to say. "I don't know."

"Do you care about him?"

Ryan didn't answer at once. She wanted to say no and shrug it off. She had no reason to care. "Yes, I do," she heard herself say. "I care about him."

"Let's go have a drink," Bess suggested and pulled on her shirt. "We'll talk."


"Champagne cocktails," Bess ordered when they slipped into a booth in the lounge. "I'm buying." She pulled out a cigarette and lit it. "Don't tell Pierce," she added with a wink. "He frowns on the use of tobacco. He's a fanatic about body care."

"Link told me he runs five miles every day."

"An old habit. Pierce rarely breaks old habits." Bess drew in smoke with a sigh. "He's always been really determined, you know? You could see it, even when he was a kid."

"You knew Pierce when he was a boy?"

"We grew up together—Pierce, Link and me." Bess glanced up at the waitress when their cocktails were served. "Run a tab," she directed and looked back at Ryan. "Pierce doesn't talk about back then, not even to Link or me. He's shut it off—or tried to."

"I thought he was trying to promote an image," Ryan murmured.

"He doesn't need to."

"No." Ryan met her eyes again. "I suppose he doesn't. Did he have a difficult childhood?"

"Oh, boy." Bess took a long drink. "And then some. He was a real puny kid."

"Pierce?" Ryan thought of the hard, muscled body and stared.

"Yeah." Bess gave a muffled version of her full-throated laugh. "Hard to belive, but true. He was small for his age, skinny as a rail. The bigger kids tormented him. They needed someone to pick on, I guess. Nobody likes growing up in an orphanage."

"Orphanage?" Ryan pounced on the last word. Studying Bess's open, friendly face, she felt a flood of sympathy. "All of you?"

"Oh, hell." Bess shrugged. Ryan's eyes were full of eloquent distress. "It wasn't so bad, really. Food, a roof over your head, plenty of company. It's not like you read about in that book, that *Oliver Twist*."

"Did you lose your parents, Bess?" Ryan asked with interest rather than the sympathy she saw was unwanted.

"When I was eight. There wasn't anybody else to take me. It was the same with Link." She continued with no trace of self-pity or regret. "People want to adopt babies, mostly. Older kids aren't placed so easily."

Lifting her drink, Ryan sipped thoughtfully. It would have been twenty years ago, before the current surge of interest in adoptable children. "What about Pierce?"

"Things were different with him. He had parents. They wouldn't sign, so he was unadoptable."

Ryan's brows creased with confusion. "But if he had parents, what was he doing in an orphanage?"

"Courts took him away from them. His father..." Bess let out a long stream of smoke. She was taking a chance, talking like this. Pierce wasn't going to like it if he found out. She could only hope it paid off. "His father used to beat his mother."

"Oh, my God!" Ryan's horrified eyes clung to Bess's. "And—and Pierce?"

"Now and again," Bess answered calmly. "But mostly his mother. First he'd hit the booze, then he'd hit his wife."

A surge of raw pain spread in the pit of her stomach. Ryan lifted her drink again. Of course she knew such things happened, but her world had always been so shielded. Her own parents might have ignored her a great deal of her life, but neither had ever lifted a hand to her. True, her father's shouting had been frightening at times, but it had never gone beyond a raised voice and impatient words. She had never dealt with physical violence of any sort firsthand. Though she tried to conceive the kind of ugliness Bess was calmly relating, it was too distant.

"Tell me," she asked finally. "I want to understand him."

It was what Bess wanted to hear. She gave Ryan a silent vote of approval and continued. "Pierce was five. This time his father beat his mother badly enough to put her in the hospital. Usually, he locked Pierce in a closet before he started on one of his rages, but this time he knocked him around a little first."

Ryan controlled the need to protest what she was hearing but kept silent. Bess watched her steadily as she spoke. "That's when the social workers took over. After the usual paper work and court hearings, his parents were judged unfit, and he was placed in the orphanage."

"Bess, his mother." Ryan shook her head, trying to think it through. "Why didn't she leave his father and take Pierce with her? What kind of woman would—"

"I'm not a psychiatrist," Bess interrupted. "As far as Pierce ever knew, she stayed with his father."

"And gave up her child," Ryan murmured. "He must have felt so completely rejected, so frightened and alone."

What sort of damage does that do to a small mind? she wondered. What sort of compensations does a child like that make? Did he escape from chains and trunks and safes because he had once been a small boy locked in a dark closet? Did he continually seek to do the impossible because he had once been so helpless?

"He was a loner," Bess continued as she ordered another round. "Maybe that's one of the reasons the other kids tormented him. At least until Link came." Bess grinned, enjoying this part of her memories. "Nobody ever touched Pierce when Link was in sight.

He's always been twice as big as anyone else. And that face!"

She laughed again, but there was nothing callous in the sound. "When Link first came, none of the other kids would go near him. Except Pierce. They were both outcasts. So was I. Link's been attached to Pierce ever since. I really don't know what might have happened to him without Pierce. Or to me."

"You really love him, don't you?" Ryan asked, drawn close in spirit to the large, exuberant redhead.

"He's my best friend," Bess answered simply. "They let me into their little club when I was ten." She smiled over the rim of her glass. "I saw Link coming and climbed up a tree. He scared me to death. We called him the Missing Link."

"Children can be cruel."

"You betcha. Anyway, just as he was passing underneath, the branch broke and I fell out. He caught me." She leaned forward, cupping her chin on her hands. "I'll never forget that. One minute I'm falling a mile a minute, and the next he's holding me. I looked up at that face and got ready to scream blue blazes. Then he laughed. I fell in love on the spot."

Ryan swallowed champagne quickly. There was no mistaking the dreamy look in Bess's eyes. "You—you and Link?"

"Well, me, anyway," Bess said ruefully. "I've been nuts about the big lug for twenty years. He still thinks I'm Little Bess. All six feet of me." She grinned and winked. "But I'm working on him."

"I thought you and Pierce..." Ryan began, then trailed off.

"Me and Pierce?" Bess let loose with one of her lusty laughs, causing heads to turn. "Are you kidding? You know enough about show business to cast better than that, sweetie. Do I look like Pierce's type?''

"Well, I..." Embarrassed by Bess's outspoken humor, Ryan shrugged. "I wouldn't have any idea what his type would be."

Bess laughed into her fresh drink. "You look smarter than that," she commented. "Anyway, he was always a quiet kid, always—what's the word?" Her forehead furrowed in thought. "Intense, you know? He had a temper." Grinning again, she rolled her eyes. "He gave a black eye for every one he got in the early days. But as he got older, he'd hold back. It was pretty clear he'd made up his mind not to follow in his old man's footsteps. When Pierce makes up his mind, that's it."

Ryan remembered the cold fury, the iced-over violence, and began to understand.

"When he was about nine, I guess, he had this accident." Bess drank, then scowled. "At least that's what he called it. He went head first down a flight of stairs. Everybody knew he'd been pushed, but he'd never say who. I think he didn't want Link to do something he could have gotten in trouble for. The fall hurt his back. They didn't think he'd walk again."

"Oh, no!"

"Yeah." Bess took another long drink. "But Pierce said he was going to walk. He was going to run five miles every day of his life."

"Five miles," Ryan murmured.

"He was determined. He worked at therapy like his life depended on it. Maybe it did," she added thoughtfully. "Maybe it did. He spent six months in the hospital."

"I see." She was seeing Pierce in the pediatric ward, giving himself to children, talking to them, making them laugh. Bringing them magic.

"While he was in, one of the nurses gave him a magic set. That was it." Bess toasted with her glass. "A five-dollar magic set. It was like he'd been waiting for it, or it was waiting for him. By the time he got out, he could do things a lot of guys in the club field have trouble with." Love and pride mingled in her voice. "He was a natural."

Ryan could see him, a dark, intense boy in a white hospital bed, perfecting, practicing, discovering.

"Listen," Bess laughed again and leaned forward. Ryan's eyes were speaking volumes. "Once when I visited him in the hospital, he set the sheet on fire." She paused as Ryan's expression became one of horror. "I swear, I *saw* it burning. Then he patted it with his hand." She demonstrated with her palm on the table. "Smoothed it out, and there was nothing. No burn, no hole, not even a singe. The little creep scared me to death."

Ryan found herself laughing despite the ordeal he must have experienced. He'd beaten it. He'd won. "To Pierce," she said and lifted her glass.

"Damn right." Bess touched rims before she tossed off the champagne. "He took off when he was sixteen. I missed him like crazy. I never thought I'd see him or Link again. I guess it was the loneliest two years of my life. Then, one day I was working in this diner in Denver, and he walks in. I don't know how he found me, he never said, but he walks in and tells me to quit. I was going to go work for him."

"Just like that?" Ryan demanded.

"Just like that."

"What did you say?"

"I didn't say anything. It was Pierce." With a smile, Bess signaled the waitress again. "I quit. We went on the road. Drink up, sweetie, you're one behind."

Ryan studied her a moment, then obliged by finishing off her drink. It wasn't every man who could command that sort of unquestioning loyalty from a strong woman. "I usually stop at two," Ryan told her, indicating the cocktail.

"Not tonight," Bess announced. "I always drink champagne when I get sentimental. You wouldn't believe some of the places we played those first years," she went on. "Kids' parties, stag parties, the works. Nobody handles a rowdy crowd like Pierce. When he looks at a guy, then whips a fireball out of his pocket, the guy quiets down."

"I imagine so," Ryan agreed and laughed at the image. "I'm not even sure he'd need the fireball."

"You got it," Bess said, pleased. "Anyway, he always knew he was going to make it, and he took Link and me along. He didn't have to. That's just the kind of man he is. He doesn't let many people in close, but the ones he does, it's forever." She stirred the champagne quietly a moment. "I know Link and me could never keep up with him up here, you know?" Bess tapped her temple. "But it doesn't matter to Pierce. We're his friends."

"I think," Ryan said slowly, "he chooses his friends very well."

Bess sent her a brilliant smile. "You're a nice lady, Ryan. A real lady, too. Pierce is the kind of man who needs a lady."

Ryan became very interested in the color of her drink. "Why do you say that?"

"Because he has class, always has. He needs a classy woman and one who's warm like he is."

"Is he warm, Bess?" Ryan's eyes came back up, searching. "Sometimes he seems so . . . distant."

"You know where he got that stupid cat?" Ryan shook her head at the question. "Somebody'd hit it and left it on the side of the road. Pierce was driving back after a week run in San Francisco. He stopped and took it to the vet. Two o'clock in the morning, and he's waking up the vet and making him operate on some stray cat. Cost him three hundred dollars. Link told me." She pulled out another cigarette. "How many people you know who'd do that?"

Ryan looked at her steadily. "Pierce wouldn't like it if he knew you'd told me all this, would he?"

"No."

"Why have you?"

Bess flashed her a smile again. "It's a trick I learned from him over the years. You look dead in somebody's eyes and you know if you can trust them."

Ryan met the look and spoke seriously. "Thank you."

"And," Bess added casually as she downed more champagne, "you're in love with him."

The words Ryan had begun to say jammed in her throat. She began coughing fitfully.

"Drink up, sweetie. Nothing like love to make you choke. Here's to it." She clinked her glass against Ryan's. "And good luck to both of us."

"Luck?" Ryan said weakly.

"With men like those two, we need it."

This time Ryan signaled for another round.

# Chapter Eight

When Ryan walked through the casino with Bess, she was laughing. The wine had lifted her mood, but more, Bess's company had cheered her. Since she had returned from school, Ryan had given herself little time to develop friendships. Finding one so quickly took her higher than the champagne.

"Celebrating?"

Both of them looked up and spotted Pierce. In unison, their faces registered the abashed guilt of children caught with one hand in the cookie jar. Pierce's brow lifted. With a laugh, Bess leaned over and kissed him enthusiastically.

"Just a little girl talk, sweetie. Ryan and I found out we have a lot in common."

"Is that so?" He watched as Ryan pressed her fingers to her mouth to stifle a giggle. It was apparent they'd had more than talk.

"Isn't he terrific when he's all serious and dry?" Bess asked Ryan. "Nobody does it better than Pierce." She kissed him again. "I didn't get your lady drunk, just maybe a little looser than she's used to. Besides, she's a big girl." Still resting her hand on his shoulder, Bess looked around. "Where's Link?"

"Watching the keno board."

"See you later." She gave Ryan a wink and was off.

"She's crazy about him, you know," Ryan said confidentially.

"Yes, I know."

She took a step closer. "Is there anything you don't know, Mr. Atkins?" She watched his lips curve at her emphasis on his surname. "I wondered if you'd ever do that for me again."

"Do what?"

"Smile. You haven't smiled at me in days."

"Haven't I?" He couldn't stop the surge of tenderness but contented himself with brushing the hair back from her face.

"No. Not once. Are you sorry?"

"Yes." Pierce steadied her with a hand on her shoulder and wished she wouldn't look at him in quite that way. He had managed to back down on needs while sharing the same set of rooms with her. Now, surrounded by noise and people and lights, he felt the force of desire building. He removed his hand. "Would you like me to take you upstairs?"

"I'm going to play blackjack," she informed him grandly. "I've wanted to for days, but I kept remembering gambling was foolish. I've just forgotten that."

Pierce held her arm as she started to walk to the table. "How much money do you have on you?"

"Oh, I don't know." Ryan rummaged in her purse. "About seventy-five dollars."

"All right." If she lost, Pierce decided, seventy-five would put no great hole in her bank account. He went with her.

"I've been watching this for days," she whispered as she took a seat at a ten-dollar table. "I've got it all figured out."

"Doesn't everyone?" he muttered and stood beside her. "Give the lady twenty dollars worth of chips," he told the dealer.

"Fifty," Ryan corrected, counting out bills.

With a nod from Pierce, the dealer exchanged the bills for colored chips.

"Are you going to play?" Ryan asked him.

"I don't gamble."

She lifted her brows. "What do you call being nailed inside a packing crate?"

He gave her one of his slow smiles. "My profession."

She laughed and sent him a teasing grin. "Do you disapprove of gambling and other vices, Mr. Atkins?"

"No." He felt another leap of desire and controlled it. "But I like to figure my own odds." He nodded as the cards were dealt. "It's never easy to beat the house at its own game."

"I feel lucky tonight," she told him.

The man beside Ryan swirled a bourbon and signed his name on a sheet of paper. He had just dropped over two thousand dollars. Philosophically, he bought another five thousand dollars worth of chips. Ryan watched a diamond glitter on his pinky as the cards were dealt. A triple deck, she remembered and lifted the tips of her own cards carefully. She saw an eight and a five. A young blonde in a black Halston took a hit and busted on twenty-three. The man with the diamond held on eighteen. Ryan took a hit and was pleased with another five. She held, then waited patiently as two more players took cards.

The dealer turned over fourteen, flipped over his next card and hit twenty. The man with the diamond swore softly as he lost another five hundred dollars.

Ryan counted her next cards, watched the hits and lost again. Undaunted, she waited for her third deal. She drew seventeen. Before she could signal the dealer she would hold, Pierce nodded for the hit.

"Wait a minute," Ryan began.

"Take it," he said simply.

With a huff and a shrug, she did. She hit twenty. Eyes wide, she swiveled in her chair to stare at him, but he was watching the cards. The dealer held on nineteen and paid her off.

"I won!" she exclaimed, pleased with the stack of chips pushed at her. "How did you know?"

He only smiled at her and continued to watch the cards.

On the next hand she drew a ten and a six. She would have taken the hit, but Pierce touched her shoulder and shook his head. Swallowing her protest, Ryan stayed pat. The dealer broke on twenty-two.

She laughed, delighted, but looked over at him again. "How do you do that?" she demanded. "It's a triple deck. You can't possibly remember all the cards dealt or figure what's left." He said nothing, and her brow creased. "Can you?"

Pierce smiled again and shook his head simply. Then he steered Ryan to another win.

"Want to take a look at mine?" the man with the diamond demanded, pushing aside his cards in disgust.

Ryan leaned toward him. "He's a sorcerer, you know. I take him everywhere."

The young blonde tucked her hair behind her ear. "I could use a spell or two myself." She sent Pierce a slow invitation. Ryan caught her eye as the cards were dealt.

"Mine," she said coolly and didn't see Pierce's brow go up. The blonde went back to her cards.

For the next hour Ryan's luck—or Pierce's—held. When the pile of chips in front of her had grown considerably, he opened her purse and swept them inside.

"Oh, but wait. I'm just getting started!"

"The secret of winning is knowing when to stop," Pierce told her and helped her off the stool. "Cash them in, Ryan, before you take it into your head to lose them at baccarat."

"But I did want to play," she began, casting a glance behind her.

"Not tonight."

With a heavy sigh she dumped the contents of her purse at the cashier's booth. Along with the chips was a comb, a lipstick and a penny that had been flattened by the wheel of a train.

"That's for luck," she said when Pierce picked it up to examine it.

"Superstition, Miss Swan," he murmured. "You surprise me."

"It's not superstition," she insisted, stuffing bills in her purse as the cashier counted them out. "It's for luck."

"I stand corrected."

"I like you, Pierce." Ryan linked her arm with his. "I thought I should tell you."

"Do you?"

"Yes," she said definitely. She could tell him that, she thought as they moved to the elevators. That was safe and certainly true. She wouldn't tell him what Bess had said so casually. *Love him?* No, that was far from safe, and it wasn't necessarily true. Even though...even though she was becoming more and more afraid it was.

"Do you like me?" Ryan turned to him and smiled as the elevator doors clicked shut.

"Yes, Ryan." He ran his knuckles over her cheek. "I like you."

"I wasn't sure." She stepped closer to him, and he felt a tingle race along his skin. "You've been angry with me."

"No, I haven't been angry with you."

She was staring up at him. Pierce could feel the air grow thick, as it did when the lid closed on him in a box or a trunk. His heart rate speeded up, and with sheer mental determination, he leveled it. He wasn't going to touch her again.

Ryan saw something flicker in his eyes. A hunger. Hers grew as well, but more, she felt a need to touch, to soothe. To love. She knew him now, though he was unaware of it. She wanted to give him something. She reached up to touch his cheek, but Pierce caught her fingers in his as the door opened.

"You must be tired," he said roughly and drew her into the corridor.

"No." Ryan laughed with the new sense of power. He was just a little afraid of her. She sensed it. Something shot into her—a combination of wine and winning and knowledge. And she wanted him.

"Are you tired, Pierce?" she asked when he unlocked the door to the suite.

"It's late."

"No. No, it's never late in Las Vegas." She tossed her purse aside and stretched. "There's no time here, don't you know? No clocks." Lifting her hair, she let it fall slowly through her fingers. "How can it be late when you don't know what time it is?" She spotted his papers on the table and crossed to them, kicking off her shoes as she went. "You work too much, Mr. Atkins." Laughing, she turned back to him. "Miss Swan's like that, isn't she?"

Her hair had tumbled over her shoulders, and her cheeks were flushed. Her eyes were alive, dancing, alluring. In them he saw that his thoughts were no secret to her. Desire was a hammer thrust in his stomach. Pierce said nothing.

"But you like Miss Swan," she murmured. "I don't always. Come sit down. Explain this to me." Ryan dropped to the couch and picked up one of his papers. It was covered with drawings and notes that made absolutely no sense to her.

Pierce moved then, telling himself it was only to keep her from disturbing his work. "It's too complicated." He took the sheet from her hand and set it back down.

"I've a very quick mind." Ryan pulled his arm until he sat beside her. She looked at him and smiled. "Do you know, the first time I looked into your eyes I thought my heart stopped." She put her hand to his cheek. "The first time you kissed me I knew it did."

Pierce caught her hand again, knowing he was close to the edge. Her free one ran up his shirtfront to his throat. "Ryan, you should go to bed."

She could hear the desire in his voice. Under her fingertip the pulse in his throat throbbed quickly. Her own heart began to match the rhythm. "No one's ever kissed me like that before," she murmured and slipped her fingers to the first button of his shirt. She freed it, watching his eyes. "No one's ever made me feel like that before. Was it magic, Pierce?'' She loosened the second and third buttons.

"No." He reached up to stop the questing fingers that were driving him mad.

"I think it was." Ryan shifted and caught his earlobe lightly between her teeth. "I know it was." The whispering breath went straight to the pit of his stomach to stoke the flames. They flared high and threatened to explode. Catching her by the shoulders, Pierce started to draw her away, but her hands were on his naked chest. Her mouth brushed his throat. His fingers tightened as the tug of war went on inside him.

"Ryan." Though he concentrated, he couldn't steady his pulse. "What are you trying to do?"

"I'm trying to seduce you," she murmured, trailing her lips down to follow her fingers. "Is it working?"

Her hands ran down his rib cage to play lightly over his stomach. She felt the quiver of response and grew bolder.

"Yes, it's working very well."

Ryan laughed, a throaty, almost mocking sound that made his blood pound. Though he didn't touch her, he was no longer able to stop her from touching him. Her hands were soft and teasing while her tongue flicked lightly at his ear.

"Are you sure?" she whispered as she slipped his shirt from his shoulders. "Maybe I'm doing something wrong." She trailed her mouth to his chin, then let her tongue run briefly over his lips. "Maybe you don't want me to touch you like this." She ran a fingertip down the center of his chest to the waist of his jeans. "Or like this." She nipped his bottom lip, still watching his eyes.

No, she'd been wrong. They were black—black, not gray. Needs drove her until she thought she would be swallowed by them. Could it be possible to want so much? So much that your whole body ached and pounded and threatened to shatter?

"I wanted you when you walked offstage tonight," she said huskily. "Right then, while I still half-believed you were a wizard and not a man. And now." She ran her hands up his chest to link them behind his neck. "Now, knowing you're a man, I want you more." She let her eyes lower to his mouth, then lifted them back to his. "But maybe you don't want me. Maybe I don't... arouse you."

"Ryan." He'd lost the ability to control his pulse, his thoughts, his concentration. He'd lost the will to try to find it again. "There won't be any turning back in a moment."

She laughed, giddy with excitement, driven by desire. She let her lips hover a breath from his. "Promise?"

Ryan exulted in the power of the kiss. His mouth was on hers fiercely, painfully. She was under him with such speed, she never felt the movement, only his hard body on hers. He was pulling at her blouse, impatient with buttons. Two flew off to land somewhere on the carpet before his hand took her breast. Ryan moaned and arched against him, desperate to be touched. His tongue went deep to tangle with hers.

Desire was white-hot—flashes of heat, splashes of color. Her skin was searing wherever he touched. She was naked without knowing how she had become so, and his bare flesh was melded to hers. His teeth were on her breast, lightly at the edge of control, then his tongue swept across her nipple until she moaned and pressed closer.

Pierce could feel the hammer beat of her pulse, almost taste it as his mouth hurried to her other breast. Her moans and her urging hands were driving him beyond reason. He was trapped in a furnace, but there would be no escape this time. He knew his flesh would melt into hers until there was nothing left to keep him separate. The heat, her scent, her taste all whirled inside his head. Excitement? No, this was more than excitement. It was obsession.

He slipped his fingers inside her. She was so soft, so warm and moist, he had no more will left.

He entered her with a wildness that stunned them both. Then she was moving with him, frantic and strong. He felt the pain of impossible pleasure, knowing he had been the enchanted, not the enchanter. He was utterly hers.

Ryan felt his ragged breath against her neck. His heart was still racing. For me, she thought dreamily as she floated on the aftermath of passion. *Mine,* she thought again and sighed. How had Bess known before she had? Ryan closed her eyes and let herself drift.

It must show on her face like a neon sign. Is it too soon to tell him? she wondered. Wait, she decided, touching his hair. She would let herself have time to get used to love before she proclaimed it. At that moment she felt she had all the time in the world.

She gave a murmured protest when Pierce took his weight from her. Slowly, she opened her eyes. He stared down at his hands. He was cursing himself steadily.

"Did I hurt you?" he demanded in a quick, rough burst.

"No," she said, surprised, then remembered Bess's story. "No, you didn't hurt me, Pierce. You couldn't. You're a very gentle man."

His eyes whipped back to hers, dark, anguished. There had been no gentleness in him when he had loved her. Only needs and desperation. "Not always," he said sharply and reached for his jeans.

"What are you doing?"

"I'll go down and get another room." He was dressing swiftly as she looked on. "I'm sorry this happened. I won't..." He stopped when he looked and saw tears welling in her eyes. Something ripped inside his stomach. "Ryan, I am sorry." Sitting beside her again, he brushed a tear away with his thumb. "I swore I wasn't going to touch you. I shouldn't have. You'd had too much to drink. I knew that and should've—"

"Damn you!" She slapped his hand away. "I was wrong. You *can* hurt me. Well, you don't have to get another room." She reached down for her blouse. "I'll get one myself. I won't stay here after you've turned something wonderful into a mistake."

She was up and tugging on her blouse, which was inside out.

"Ryan, I—"

"Oh, shut up!" Seeing the two middle buttons were missing, she tore the blouse off again and stood facing him, haughtily naked, eyes blazing. He nearly pulled her to the floor and took her again. "I knew exactly what I was doing, do you hear? Exactly! If you think it only takes a few drinks to make me throw myself at a man, then you're wrong. I wanted you, I thought you wanted me. So if it was a mistake, it was yours."

"It wasn't a mistake for me, Ryan." His voice had softened, but when he reached out to touch her, she jerked back. He let his hand drop to his side and chose his words carefully. "I wanted you; perhaps, I thought, too much. And I wasn't as gentle with you as I wanted to be. It's difficult for me to deal with knowing I couldn't stop myself from having you."

For a moment she studied him, then brushed tears away with the back of her hand. "Did you want to stop yourself?"

"The point is, I tried and couldn't. And I've never taken a woman with less..." He hesitated. "Care," he murmured. "You're very small, very fragile."

Fragile? she thought and lifted a brow. No one had ever called her that before. At another time she might have enjoyed it, but now she felt there was only one way to handle a man like Pierce. "Okay," she told him and took a deep breath. "You've got two choices."

Surprised, Pierce drew his brows together. "What are they?"

"You can get yourself another room or you can take me to bed and make love to me again." She took a step toward him. "Right now."

He met the challenge in her eyes and smiled. "Those are my only choices?"

"I suppose I could seduce you again if you want to be stubborn," she said with a shrug. "It's up to you."

He let his fingers dive into her hair as he drew her closer. "What if we combined two of those choices?"

She gave him a look of consideration. "Which two?"

He lowered his mouth to hers for a soft, lingering kiss. "How about I take you to bed and you seduce me?"

Ryan allowed him to lift her into his arms. "I'm a reasonable person," she agreed as he walked to the bedroom. "I'm willing to discuss a compromise as long as I get my own way."

"Miss Swan," Pierce murmured as he laid her gently on the bed. "I like your style."

# Chapter Nine

Ryan's body ached. Sighing, she snuggled deeper into the pillow. It was a pleasant discomfort. It reminded her of the night—the night that had lasted until dawn.

She hadn't known she had so much passion to give or so many needs to fill. Each time she had thought herself drained, body and mind, she had only to touch him again, or he her. Strength would flood back into her, and with it the unrelenting demands of desire.

Then they had slept, holding each other as the rosy tones of sunrise had slipped into the room. Drifting awake, clinging to sleep, Ryan shifted toward Pierce, wanting to hold him again.

She was alone.

Confusion had her eyes slowly opening. Sliding her hand over the sheets beside her, Ryan found them cold. *Gone?* she thought hazily. How long had she been sleeping alone? All of her dreamy pleasure died. Ryan touched the sheets again. No, she told herself and stretched, he's just in the other room. He wouldn't have left me alone.

The phone shrilled and jolted her completely awake.

"Yes, hello." She answered it on the first ring and pushed her hair from her face with her free hand. *Why was the suite so quiet?*

"Miss Swan?"

"Yes, this is Ryan Swan."

"Bennett Swan calling, please hold."

Ryan sat up, automatically pulling the sheets to her breast. Disoriented, she wondered what time it was. And where, she thought again, was Pierce?

"Ryan, give me an update."

An update? she repeated silently, hearing her father's voice. She struggled to put her thoughts into order.

"Ryan!"

"Yes, I'm sorry."

"I haven't got all day."

"I've watched Pierce's rehearsals daily," she began, wishing for a cup of coffee and a few moments to pull herself together. "I think you'll find he has the technical areas and his own crew well in hand." She glanced around the bedroom, looking for some sign of him. "He opened last night, flawlessly. We've already discussed some alterations for the special, but nothing's firmed up as yet. At this point whatever new routines he's worked out he's keeping to himself."

"I want some firm estimates on the set within two weeks," he told her. "We might have a change in the scheduling. You work it out with Atkins. I want a list of his proposed routines and the time allowance for each one."

"I've already discussed it with him," Ryan said coolly, annoyed that her father was infringing on her territory. "I am the producer, aren't I?"

"You are," he agreed. "I'll see you in my office when you get back."

Hearing the click, Ryan hung up with a sigh of exasperation. It had been a typical Bennett Swan conversation. She pushed the phone call from her mind and scrambled from the bed. Pierce's robe lay draped over a chair, and picking it up, Ryan slipped it on.

"Pierce?" Ryan hurried out into the living area of the suite but found it empty. "Pierce?" she called again, stepping on one of the lost buttons from her blouse. Absently, Ryan picked it up and dropped it in the pocket of the robe before she walked through the suite.

Empty. The pain started in her stomach and spread. He had left her alone. Shaking her head, Ryan searched the rooms again. He must have left her a note telling her why and where he'd gone. He wouldn't just wake up and leave her, not after last night.

But there was nothing. Ryan shivered, suddenly cold.

It was the pattern of her life, she decided. Moving to the window, she stared out at unlit neon. Whoever she cared for, whoever she gave love to, always went their own way. Yet somehow, she still expected it to be different.

When she had been small, it had been her mother, a young, glamour-loving woman jetting off to follow Bennett Swan all over the world. *You're a big girl, Ryan, and so self-sufficient. I'll be back in a few days.* Or a few weeks, Ryan remembered. There had always been a housekeeper and other servants to see that she was tended to. No, she had never been neglected or abused. Just forgotten.

Later it had been her father, dashing here and there at a moment's notice. But of course, he'd seen that she had had a solid, dependable nanny whom he had paid a very substantial salary. Then she'd been shipped off to Switzerland, the best boarding school available. *That daughter of mine has a head on her shoulders. Top ten percent of her class.*

There'd always been an expensive present on her birthday with a card from thousands of miles away telling her to keep up the good work. Of course, she had. She would never have risked disappointing him.

Nothing ever changes, Ryan thought as she turned to stare at herself in the mirror. Ryan's strong. Ryan's practical. Ryan doesn't need all the things other women do—hugs, gentleness, romance.

They're right, of course, she told herself. It's foolish to be hurt. We wanted each other. We spent the night together. Why romanticize it? I don't have any claim on Pierce. And he has none on me. She fingered the lapel of his robe, then quickly dropped her hand. Moving swiftly, Ryan stripped and went to shower.

Ryan kept the water almost unbearably hot, allowing it to beat full force against her skin. She wasn't going to think. She knew herself well. If she kept her mind a blank, when she opened it again, she'd know what she had to do.

The air in the bath was steamy and moist when she stepped out to towel herself. Her moves were brisk again. There was work to be done—notes to write on ideas and plans. Ryan Swan, Executive Producer. That's what she had to concentrate on. It was time to stop worrying about the people who couldn't—or wouldn't—give her what she wanted. She had a name to make for herself in the industry. That was all that really mattered.

As she dressed, she was perfectly calm. Dreams were for sleeping, and she was wide awake. There were dozens of details to be seen to. She had meetings to set up, department heads to deal with. Decisions had to be made. She had been in Las Vegas long enough. She knew Pierce's style as well as she ever would. And, more important to her at the moment, she knew precisely what she wanted in the finished product. Back in Los Angeles, Ryan could start putting her ideas into motion.

It was going to be her first production, but she'd be damned if it was going to be her last. This time she had places of her own to go to.

Ryan picked up her comb and ran it through her damp hair. The door opened behind her.

"So, you're awake." Pierce smiled and started to cross to her. The look in her eyes stopped him. Angry hurt—he could feel waves of it.

"Yes, I'm awake," she said easily and continued to comb her hair. "I've been up for some time. My father called earlier. He wanted a progress report."

"Oh?" Her emotions weren't directed toward her father, Pierce decided, watching her steadily. "Have you ordered anything from room service?"

"No."

"You'll want some breakfast," he said, taking another step toward her. He went no farther, feeling the wall she had thrown up between them.

"No, actually, I don't." Ryan took out her mascara and began to apply it with great care. "I'll get some coffee at the airport. I'm going back to L.A. this morning."

The cool, matter-of-fact tone had his stomach muscles tightening. Could he have been so wrong? Had the night they had shared meant so little to her? "This morning?" he repeated, matching her tone. "Why?"

"I think I have a fairly good handle on how you work and what you'll want for the special." She kept her eyes focused only on her own in the mirror. "I should start on the preliminary stages, then we can set up a meeting when you're back in California. I'll call your agent."

Pierce bit off the words he wanted to say. He never put chains on anyone but himself. "If that's what you want."

Ryan's fingers tightened on the tube of mascara before she set it down. "We both have our jobs to do. Mine's in L.A., yours, for the moment, is here." She turned to go to the closet, but he laid a hand on her shoulder. Pierce dropped it immediately when she stiffened.

"Ryan, have I hurt you?"

"Hurt me?" she repeated and continued on to the closet. Her tone was like a shrug, but he couldn't see her eyes. "How could you have possibly hurt me?"

"I don't know." He spoke from directly behind her. Ryan pulled out an armful of clothes. "But I have." He turned her to face him. "I can see it in your eyes."

"Forget it," she told him. "I will." She started to walk away, but this time he kept his hands firm.

"I can't forget something unless I know what it is." Though he kept his hands light, annoyance had crept into his tone. "Ryan, tell me what's wrong."

"Drop it, Pierce."

"No."

Ryan tried to jerk away again, and again he held her still. She told herself to be calm. "You *left* me!" she exploded and tossed the clothes aside. The passion erupted from her so swiftly, it left him staring and speechless. "I woke up and you were gone, without a word. I'm not used to one-night stands."

His eyes kindled at that. "Ryan—"

"No, I don't want to hear it." She shook her head vigorously. "I expected something different from you.

I was wrong. But that's all right. A woman like me doesn't need all the niceties. I'm an expert on surviving.'' She twisted but found herself held against him. ''Don't! Let me go, I have to pack.''

''Ryan.'' Even as she resisted, he held her closer. The hurt went deep, he thought, and hadn't started with him. ''I'm sorry.''

''I want you to let me go, Pierce.''

''You won't listen to me if I do.'' He stroked a hand down her wet hair. ''I need you to listen.''

''There's nothing to say.''

Her voice had thickened, and he felt a wicked stab of self-blame. How could he have been so stupid? How could he not have seen what would be important to her?

''Ryan, I know a lot about one-night stands.'' Pierce drew her away, just far enough so that he could see her eyes. ''That isn't what last night was for me.''

She shook her head fiercely, struggling for composure. ''There's no need for you to say that.''

''I told you once, I don't lie, Ryan.'' He slipped his hands up to her shoulders. ''What we had together last night is very important to me.''

''You were gone when I woke up.'' She swallowed and shut her eyes. ''The bed was cold.''

''I'm sorry. I went down to smooth out a few things before tonight's show.''

''If you'd woke me—''

''I never thought to wake you, Ryan,'' he said quietly. ''Just as I never thought how you might feel waking up alone. The sun was coming in when you fell asleep.''

"You were up as long as I was." She tried to turn away again. "Pierce, *please!*" Hearing the desperation in the word, she bit her lip. "Let me go."

He lowered his hands, then watched as she gathered her clothes again. "Ryan, I never sleep more than five or six hours. It's all I need." Was this panic he was feeling watching her fold a blouse into a suitcase? "I thought you'd still be sleeping when I got back."

"I reached for you," she said simply. "And you were gone."

"Ryan—"

"No, it doesn't matter." She pressed her hands to her temples a moment and let out a deep breath. "I'm sorry. I'm acting like a fool. You haven't done anything, Pierce. It's me. I always expect too much. I'm always floored when I don't get it." Quickly, she began to pack again. "I didn't mean to make a scene. Please forget it."

"It isn't something I want to forget," he murmured.

"I'd feel less foolish if I knew you would," she said, trying to make her voice light. "Just put it down to a lack of sleep and a bad disposition. I should be going back, though. I've a lot of work to do."

He had seen her needs from the first—her response to gentleness, her pleasure in the gift of a flower. She was an emotional, romantic woman who tried very hard not to be. Pierce cursed himself, thinking how she must have felt to find the bed empty after the night they had spent together.

"Ryan, don't go." That was difficult for him. It was something he never asked of anyone.

Her fingers hesitated at the locks of her suitcase. Clicking them shut, Ryan set it on the floor, then turned. "Pierce, I'm not angry, honestly. A little embarrassed, maybe." She managed a smile. "I really should go back and start things moving. There might be a change in the scheduling, and—"

"Stay," he interrupted, unable to stop himself. "Please."

Ryan remained silent a moment. Something she saw in his eyes had a block lodging in her throat. It was costing him something to ask. Just as it was going to cost her something to ask. "Why?"

"I need you." He took a breath after what was for him a staggering admission. "I don't want to lose you."

Ryan took a step toward him. "Does it matter?"

"Yes. Yes, it matters."

She waited for a moment but was unable to convince herself to walk out the door. "Show me," she told him.

Going to her, he gathered her close. Ryan shut her eyes. It was exactly what she had needed—to be held, just to be held. His chest was firm against her cheek, his arms strong around her. Yet she knew she was being held as if she were something precious. Fragile, he had called her. For the first time in her life, Ryan wanted to be.

"Oh, Pierce, I'm an idiot."

"No." He lifted her chin with a finger and kissed her. "You're very sweet." He smiled then and laid his forehead on hers. "Are you going to complain when I wake you up after five hours sleep?"

"Never." Laughing, she threw her arms around his neck. "Or maybe just a little."

She smiled at him, but his eyes were suddenly serious. Pierce slid a hand up to cup the back of her neck before his mouth lowered to hers.

It was like the first time—the gentleness, the featherlight pressure that turned her blood to flame. She was utterly helpless when he kissed her like this, unable to pull him closer, unable to demand. She could only let him take in his own time.

Pierce knew that this time the power was his alone. It made his hands move tenderly as they undressed her. He let her blouse slip slowly off her shoulders, down her back, to flutter to the floor. Her skin quivered as his hands passed over it.

Unhooking her trousers, he drew them down her hips, letting his fingers toy with the tiny swatch of silk and lace that rose high at her thighs. All the while his mouth nibbled at hers. Her breath caught, then she moaned as he trailed a finger inside the silk. But he didn't remove it. Instead, he slid his hand to her breast to stroke and tease until she began to tremble.

"I want you," she said shakily. "Do you know how much I want you?"

"Yes." He brushed soft, butterfly kisses over her face. "Yes."

"Make love to me," Ryan whispered. "Pierce, make love to me."

"I am," he murmured and pressed his mouth to the frantic pulse in her neck.

"Now," she demanded, too weak to pull him to her.

He laughed, deep in his throat, and lowered her to the bed. "You drove me mad last night, Miss Swan, touching me like this." Pierce trailed a finger down the center of her body, stopping to linger at the soft mound between her legs. Slowly, lazily, he took his mouth to follow the trail.

In the night a madness had been on him. He had known impatience, desperation. He had taken her again and again, passionately, but had been unable to savor. It was as though he had been starved, and greed had driven him. Now, though he wanted her no less, he could restrain the need. He could taste and sample and enjoy.

Ryan's limbs were heavy. She couldn't move them, could only let him touch and caress and kiss wherever he wished. The strength that had driven her the night before had been replaced by a honeyed weakness. She lay steeped in it.

His mouth loitered at her waist, his tongue circling lower while he ran his hands lightly over her, tracing the shape of her breasts, stroking her neck and shoulders. He teased rather than possessed, aroused rather than fulfilled.

He caught the waistband of the silk in his teeth and took it inches lower. Ryan arched and moaned. But it was the skin of her thigh he tasted, savoring until she knew madness was only a breath away. She heard herself sighing his name, a soft, urgent sound, but he made no answer. His mouth was busy doing wonderful things to the back of her knee.

Ryan felt the heated skin of his chest brush over her leg, though she had no idea how or when he had rid himself of his shirt. She had never been more aware of her own body. She learned of the drugging, heavenly pleasure that could come from the touch of a fingertip on the skin.

He was lifting her, Ryan thought mistily, though her back was pressed into the bed. He was levitating her, making her float. He was showing her magic, but this trance was no illusion.

They were both naked now, wrapped together as his mouth journeyed back to hers. He kissed her slowly, deeply, until she was limp. His nimble fingers aroused. She hadn't known passion could pull two ways at once—into searing fire and into the clouds.

Her breath was heaving, but still he waited. He would give her everything first, every dram of pleasure, every dark delight he knew. Her skin was like water in his hands, flowing, rippling. He nibbled and sucked gently on her swollen lips and waited for her final moan of surrender.

"Now, love?" he asked, spreading light, whispering kisses over her face. "Now?"

She couldn't answer. She was beyond words and reason. That was where he wanted her. Exhilarated, he laughed and pressed his mouth to her throat. "You're mine, Ryan. Tell me. Mine."

"Yes." It came out on a husky breath, barely audible. "Yours." But his mouth swallowed the words even as she said them. "Take me." She didn't hear herself say it. She thought the demand was only in her brain, but then he was inside her. Ryan gasped and arched to meet him. And still he moved with painful slowness.

The blood was roaring in her ears as he drew the ultimate pleasure to its fullest. His lips rubbed over hers, capturing each trembling breath.

Abruptly, he crushed his mouth on hers—no more gentleness, no more teasing. She cried out as he took her with a sudden, wild fury. The fire consumed them both, fusing skin and lips until Ryan thought they both had died.

Pierce lay on her, resting his head between her breasts. Under his ear he heard the thunder of her heartbeat. She had yet to stop trembling. Her arms were twined around him, with one hand still tangled in his hair. He didn't want to move. He wanted to keep her like this—alone, naked, his. The fierce desire for possession shook him. It wasn't his way. Had never been his way before Ryan. The drive was too strong to resist.

"Tell me again," he demanded, lifting his face to watch hers.

Ryan's eyes opened slowly. She was drugged with love, sated with pleasure. "Tell you what?"

His mouth came to hers again, seeking, then lingered to draw the last taste. When he lifted it, his eyes were dark and demanding. "Tell me that you're mine, Ryan."

"Yours," she murmured as her eyes closed again. She sighed into sleep. "For as long as you want me."

Pierce frowned at her answer and started to speak, but her breathing was slow and even. Shifting, he lay beside her and pulled her close.

This time he would wait until she woke.

# Chapter Ten

Ryan had never known time to pass so quickly. She should have been glad of it. When Pierce's Las Vegas engagement was over, they could begin work on the special. It was something she was eager to do, for herself and for him. She knew it could be the turning point of her career.

Yet she found herself wishing the hours wouldn't fly by. There was something fanciful about Vegas, with its lack of time synchronization, its honky-tonk streets and glittery casinos. There, with the touch of magic all around, it seemed natural to love him, to share the life he lived. Ryan wasn't certain it would be so simple once they returned to the practical world.

They were both taking each day at a time. There was no talk of the future. Pierce's burst of possessiveness had never reoccurred, and Ryan wondered at it. She nearly believed she had dreamed those deep, insistent words—*You're mine. Tell me.*

He had never demanded again, nor had he given her any words of love. He was gentle, at times achingly so, with words or looks or gestures. But he was never completely free with her. Nor was Ryan ever completely free with him. Trusting came easily to neither of them.

\* \* \*

On closing night Ryan dressed carefully. She wanted a special evening. Champagne, she decided as she slipped into a frothy dress in a rainbow of hues. She would order champagne to be sent up to the suite after the performance. They had one long, last night to spend together before the idyll ended.

Ryan studied herself critically in the mirror. The dress was sheer and much more daring, she noted, than her usual style. Pierce would say it was more Ryan than Miss Swan, she thought and laughed. He would be right, as always. At the moment she didn't feel at all like Miss Swan. Tomorrow would be soon enough for business suits.

She dabbed perfume on her wrists, then at the hollow between her breasts.

"Ryan, if you want dinner before the show, you'll have to hurry along. It's nearly..." Pierce broke off as he came into the room. He stopped to stare at her. The dress floated here, clung there, wisping enticingly over her breasts in colors that melded and ran like a painting left in the rain.

"You're so lovely," he murmured, feeling the familiar thrill along his skin. "Like something I might have dreamed."

When he spoke like that, he had her heart melting and her pulse racing at the same time. "A dream?" Ryan walked to him and slid her arms around his neck. "What sort of a dream would you like me to be?" She kissed one cheek, then the other. "Will you conjure a dream for me, Pierce?"

"You smell of jasmine." He buried his face in her neck. He thought he had never wanted anything—anyone—so much in his life. "It drives me mad."

"A woman's spell." Ryan tilted her head to give his mouth more freedom. "To enchant the enchanter."

"It works."

She gave a throaty laugh and pressed closer. "Wasn't it a woman's spell that was Merlin's undoing in the end?"

"Have you been researching?" he asked in her ear.

"Careful, I've been in the business longer than you." Lifting his face, he touched his lips to hers. "It isn't wise to tangle with a magician, you know."

"I'm not in the least wise." She let her fingers run up the back of his neck, then through the thick mane of his hair. "Not in the least."

He felt a wave of power—and a wave of weakness. It was always the same when she was in his arms. Pierce pulled her close again just to hold her. Sensing some struggle, Ryan remained passive. He had so much to give, she thought, so much emotion he would offer or hold back. She could never be sure which he would choose to do. Yet wasn't it the same with her? she asked herself. She loved him but hadn't been able to say the words aloud. Even as the love grew, she still wasn't able to say them.

"Will you be in the wings tonight?" he asked her. "I like knowing you're there."

"Yes." Ryan tilted back her head and smiled. It was so rare for him to ask anything of her. "One of these days I'm going to spot something. Even *your* hand isn't always quicker than the eye."

"No?" He grinned, amused at her continued determination to catch him. "About dinner," he began and toyed with the zipper at the back of her dress. He was beginning to wonder what she wore under it. If he chose, he could have the dress on the floor at her feet before she could draw a breath.

"What about it?" she asked with a gleam of mischief in her eyes.

The knock at the door had him swearing.

"Why don't you turn whoever it is into a toad?" Ryan suggested. Then, sighing, she rested her head on his shoulder. "No, that would be rude, I suppose."

"I rather like the idea."

She laughed and drew back. "I'll answer it. I can't have that on my conscience." Toying with his top button, she lifted a brow. "You won't forget what you were thinking about while I'm sending them away?"

He smiled. "I have a very good memory." Pierce let her go and watched her walk away. Miss Swan hadn't picked out that dress, he decided, echoing Ryan's earlier thoughts.

"Package for you, Miss Swan."

Ryan accepted the small plainly wrapped box and the card from the messenger. "Thank you." After closing the door, she set down the package and opened the envelope. The note was brief and typewritten.

Ryan,

   Your report in good order. Expect a thorough briefing on Atkins project on your return. First full meeting scheduled one week from today. Happy birthday.

                              Your Father

Ryan read it over twice, then glanced briefly at the package. He wouldn't miss my birthday, she thought as she scanned the typed words a third time. Bennett Swan always did his duty. Ryan felt a surge of disappointment, of anger, of futility. All the familiar emotions of Swan's only child.

Why? she demanded of herself. Why hadn't he waited and given her something in person? Why had he sent an impersonal note that read like a telegram and a proper token his secretary no doubt selected? Why couldn't he have just sent his love?

"Ryan?" Pierce watched her from the doorway of the bedroom. He had seen her read the note. He had seen the look of emptiness in her eyes. "Bad news?"

"No." Quickly, Ryan shook her head and slipped the note into her purse. "No, it's nothing. Let's go to dinner, Pierce. I'm starving."

She was smiling, reaching out her hand for his, but the hurt in her eyes was unmistakable. Saying nothing, Pierce took her hand. As they left the suite, he glanced at the package she had never opened.

As Pierce had requested, Ryan watched the show from the wings. She had blocked all thoughts of her father from her mind. It was her last night of complete freedom, and Ryan was determined to let nothing spoil it.

It's my birthday, she reminded herself. I'm going to have my own private celebration. She had said nothing to Pierce, initially because she had forgotten her birthday entirely until her father's note had arrived. Now, she decided, it would be foolish to mention it. She was twenty-seven, after all, too old to be sentimental about the passing of a year.

"You were wonderful, as always," she told Pierce as he walked offstage, applause thundering after him. "When are you going to tell me how you do that last illusion?"

"Magic, Miss Swan, has no explanation."

She narrowed her eyes at him. "I happen to know that Bess is in her dressing room right now, and that the panther—"

"Explanations disappoint," he interrupted. He took her hand to lead her into his own dressing room. "The mind's a paradox, Miss Swan."

"Do tell," she said dryly, knowing full well he was going to explain nothing.

He managed to keep his face seriously composed as he stripped off his shirt. "The mind wants to believe the impossible," he continued as he went into the bath to wash. "Yet it doesn't. Therein lies the fascination. If the impossible is *not* possible, then how was it done before your eyes and under your nose?"

"That's what I want to know," Ryan complained over the sound of running water. When he came back in, a towel slung over his shoulder, she shot him a straight, uncompromising look. "As your producer in this special, I should—"

"Produce," he finished and pulled on a fresh shirt. "I'll do the impossible."

"It's maddening not to know," she said darkly but did up the buttons of his shirt herself.

"Yes." Pierce only smiled when she glared at him.

"It's just a trick," Ryan said with a shrug, hoping to annoy him.

"Is it?" His smile remained infuriatingly amiable.

Knowing defeat when faced with it, Ryan sighed. "I suppose you'd suffer all sorts of torture and never breathe a word."

"Did you have some in mind?"

She laughed then and pressed her mouth to his. "That's just the beginning," she promised dangerously. "I'm going to take you upstairs and drive you crazy until you talk."

"Interesting." Pierce slipped an arm around her shoulders and led her into the corridor. "It could take quite a bit of time."

"I'm in no hurry," she said blithely.

They rode to the top floor, but when Pierce started to slip the key into the lock of the suite, Ryan laid her hand on his. "This is your last chance before I get tough," she warned. "I'm going to make you talk."

He only smiled at her and pushed the door open.

*"Happy birthday!"*

Ryan's eyes widened in surprise. Bess, still in costume, opened a bottle of champagne while Link did his best to catch the spurt of wine in a glass. Speechless, Ryan stared at them.

"Happy birthday, Ryan." Pierce kissed her lightly.

"But how..." She broke off to look up at him. "How did you know?"

"Here you go." Bess stuck a glass of champagne in Ryan's hand, then gave her a quick squeeze. "Drink up, sweetie. You only get one birthday a year. Thank God. The champagne's from me—a bottle for now and one for later." She winked at Pierce.

"Thank you." Ryan looked helplessly into her glass. "I don't know what to say."

"Link's got something for you, too," Bess told her.

The big man shifted uncomfortably as all eyes turned to him. "I got you a cake," he mumbled, then cleared his throat. "You have to have a birthday cake."

Ryan walked over to see a sheet cake decorated in delicate pinks and yellows. "Oh, Link! It's lovely."

"You have to cut the first piece," he instructed.

"Yes, I will in a minute." Reaching up, Ryan drew his head down until she could reach it on tiptoe. She pressed a kiss on his mouth. "Thank you, Link."

He turned pink, grinned, then sent Bess an agonized look. "Welcome."

"I have something for you." Still smiling, Ryan turned to Pierce. "Will you kiss me, too?" he demanded.

"After I get my present."

"Greedy," he decided and handed her a small wooden box.

It was old and carved. Ryan ran her finger over it to feel the places that had worn smooth with age and handling. "It's beautiful," she murmured. She opened it and saw a tiny silver symbol on a chain. "Oh!"

"An ankh," Pierce told her, slipping it out to fasten it around her neck. "An Egyptian symbol of life. Not a superstition," he said gravely. "It's for luck."

"Pierce." Remembering her flattened penny, Ryan laughed and threw her arms around him. "Don't you ever forget anything?"

"No. Now you owe me a kiss."

Ryan complied, then forgot there were eyes on them.

"Hey, look, we want some of this cake. Don't we, Link?" Bess slipped an arm around his thick waist and grinned as Ryan surfaced.

"Will it taste as good as it looks?" Ryan wondered aloud as she picked up the knife and sliced through it. "I don't know how long it's been since I've eaten birthday cake. Here, Link, you have the first piece." Ryan licked icing from her finger as he took it. "Terrific," she judged, then began to cut another slice. "I don't know how you found out. I'd forgotten myself until…" Ryan stopped cutting and straightened. "You read my note!'' she accused Pierce. He looked convincingly blank.

"What note?"

She let out an impatient breath, not noticing that Bess had taken the knife and was slicing the cake herself. "You went in my purse and read that note."

"Went in your purse?" Pierce repeated, lifting a brow. "Really, Ryan, would I do something so crude?"

She thought about that for a moment. "Yes, you would."

Bess snickered, but he only sent her a mild glance. He accepted a piece of cake. "A magician doesn't need to stoop to picking pockets to gather information."

Link laughed, a deep rumbling sound that caught Ryan by surprise. "Like the time you lifted that guy's keys in Detroit?" he reminded Pierce.

"Or the earrings from the lady in Flatbush," Bess put in. "Nobody's got a smoother touch than you, Pierce."

"Really?" Ryan drew out the word as she looked back at him. Pierce bit into a piece of cake and said nothing.

"He always gives them back at the end of the show," Bess went on. "Good thing Pierce didn't decide on a life of crime. Think of what would happen if he started cracking safes from the outside instead of the inside."

"Fascinating," Ryan agreed, narrowing her eyes at him. "I'd love to hear more about it."

"How about the time you broke out of that little jail in Wichita, Pierce?" Bess continued obligingly. "You know when they locked you up for—"

"Have some more champagne, Bess," Pierce suggested, lifting the bottle and tilting it into her glass.

Link let out another rumbling laugh. "Sure would liked to've seen that sheriff's face when he looked in and saw an empty cell, all locked up and tidy."

"Jail-breaking," Ryan mused, fascinated.

"Houdini did it routinely." Pierce handed her a glass of champagne.

"Yeah, but he worked it out with the cops first." Bess chuckled at the look Pierce sent her and cut Link another piece of cake.

"Picking pockets, breaking jail." Ryan enjoyed the faint discomfort she saw in Pierce's eyes. It wasn't often she had him at a disadvantage. "Are there any other things I should know about?"

"It would seem you know too much already," he commented.

"Yes." She kissed him soundly. "And it's the best birthday present I've ever had."

"Come on, Link." Bess lifted the half-empty bottle of champagne. "Let's go finish this and your cake. We'll leave Pierce to work his way out of this one. You ought to tell her the one about that salesman in Salt Lake City."

"Good night, Bess," Pierce said blandly and earned another chuckle.

"Happy birthday, Ryan." Bess gave Pierce a flashing grin as she pulled Link out of the room.

"Thank you, Bess. Thank you, Link." Ryan waited until the door shut before she looked back at Pierce. "Before we discuss the salesman in Salt Lake City, why were you in a little cell in Wichita?" Her eyes laughed at him over the rim of her glass.

"A misunderstanding."

"That's what they all say." Her brow arched. "A jealous husband, perhaps?"

"No, an annoyed deputy who found himself locked to a bar stool with his own handcuffs." Pierce shrugged. "He wasn't appreciative when I let him go."

Ryan smothered a laugh. "No, I imagine he wasn't."

"A small wager," Pierce added. "He lost."

"Then instead of paying off," Ryan concluded, "he tossed you in jail."

"Something like that."

"A desperate criminal." Ryan heaved a sigh. "I suppose I'm at your mercy." Setting down her glass, she went to him. "It was very sweet of you to do this for me. Thank you."

Pierce brushed back her hair. "Such a serious face," he murmured and kissed her eyes shut. He thought of the hurt he had seen in them when she had read her father's letter. "Aren't you going to open the present from your father, Ryan?"

She shook her head, then laid her cheek on his shoulder. "No, not tonight. Tomorrow. I've been given the presents that matter already."

"He didn't forget you, Ryan."

"No, he wouldn't forget. It would be marked on his calendar. Oh, I'm sorry." She shook her head again, drawing away. "That was petty. I've always wanted too much. He does love me—in his own way."

Pierce took her hands in his. "He only knows his own way."

Ryan looked back up at him. Her frown cleared into an expression of understanding. "Yes, you're right. I've never thought about it that way. I keep struggling to please him so he'll turn to me one day and say, 'Ryan, I love you. I'm proud to be your father.' It's silly." She sighed. "I'm a grown woman, but I keep waiting."

"We don't ever stop wanting that from our parents." Pierce drew her close again.

Ryan thought of his childhood while he wondered about hers.

"We'd be different people, wouldn't we, if our parents had acted differently?"

"Yes," he answered. "We would."

Ryan tilted her head back. "I wouldn't want you to be any different, Pierce. You're exactly what I want." Hungrily, she pressed her mouth to his. "Take me to bed," she whispered. "Tell me what you were thinking all those hours ago before we were interrupted."

Pierce swept her up, and she clung, delighting in the strength of his arms. "Actually," he began, crossing to the bedroom, "I was wondering what you had on under that dress."

Ryan laughed and pressed her mouth to his throat. "Well, there's hardly anything there to wonder about at all."

The bedroom was dark and quiet as Ryan lay curled up at Pierce's side. His fingers played absently with her hair. He thought she was sleeping; she was very still. He didn't mind his own wakefulness. It allowed him to enjoy the feel of her skin against his, the silken texture of her hair. While she slept, he could touch her without arousing her, only to comfort himself that she was there. He didn't like knowing she wouldn't be in his bed the following night.

"What are you thinking about?" she murmured and startled him.

"About you." He drew her closer. "I thought you were sleeping."

"No." He felt the brush of her lashes on his shoulder as she opened her eyes. "I was thinking about you." Lifting her finger, she traced it along his jawline. "Where did you get this scar?"

He didn't answer immediately. Ryan realized she'd unwittingly probed into his past. "I suppose it was in a battle with a sorceress," she said lightly, wishing she could take the question back.

"Not quite so romantic. I fell down some stairs when I was a kid."

She held her breath a moment. She hadn't expected him to volunteer anything on his past, even so small a detail. Shifting, she rested her head on his chest. "I tripped over a stool once and loosened a tooth. My father was furious when he found out. I was terrified it would fall out and he'd disown me."

"Did he frighten you so much?"

"His disapproval, yes. I suppose it was foolish."

"No." Staring up at the dark ceiling, Pierce continued to stroke her hair. "We're all afraid of something."

"Even you?" she asked with a half-laugh. "I don't believe you're afraid of anything."

"Of not being able to get out once I'm in," he murmured.

Surprised, Ryan looked up and caught the gleam of his eyes in the darkness. "Do you mean in one of your escapes?"

"What?" He brought his thoughts back to her. He hadn't realized he had spoken aloud.

"Why do you do the escapes if you feel that way?"

"Do you think that if you ignore a fear it goes away?" he asked her. "When I was small," he said calmly, "it was a closet, and I couldn't get out. Now it's a steamer trunk or a vault, and I can escape."

"Oh, Pierce." Ryan turned her face into his chest. "I'm sorry. You don't have to talk about it."

But he was compelled to. For the first time since his childhood, Pierce heard himself speak of it. "Do you know, I think that the memory of scent stays with you longer than anything else. I could always remember the scent of my father so clearly. It wasn't until ten years after I last saw him that I learned what it was. He smelled of gin. I couldn't have told you what he looked like, but I remembered that smell."

He continued to stare up at the ceiling as he spoke. Ryan knew he had forgotten her as he went back into his own past. "One night when I was about fifteen, I was down in the cellars. I used to like to explore down there when everyone was in bed. I came across the janitor passed out in a corner with a bottle of gin. That smell—I remember being terrified for a moment without having any idea why. But I went over and picked up the bottle, and then I knew. I stopped being afraid."

Pierce was silent for a long time, and Ryan said nothing. She waited, wanting him to continue yet knowing she couldn't ask him to. The room was quiet but for the sound of his heart beating under her ear.

"He was a very cruel, very sick man," Pierce murmured, and she knew he spoke again of his father. "For years I was certain that meant I had the same sickness."

Gripping him tighter, Ryan shook her head. "There's nothing cruel in you," she whispered. "Nothing."

"Would you think so if I told you where I came from?" he wondered. "Would you be willing to let me touch you then?"

Ryan lifted her head and swallowed tears. "Bess told me a week ago," she said steadily. "And I'm here." He said nothing, but she felt his hand fall away from her hair. "You have no right to be angry with her. She's the most loyal, the most loving woman I've ever met. She told me because she knew I cared, knew I needed to understand you."

He was very still. "When?"

"The night..." Ryan hesitated and took a breath. "Opening night." She wished she could see his expression, but the darkness cloaked it. "You said we'd be lovers when I knew you," she reminded him. "You were right." Because her voice trembled, she swallowed. "Are you sorry?"

It seemed to her an eternity before he answered. "No." Pierce drew her down to him again. "No." He kissed her temple. "How could I be sorry to be your lover?"

"Then don't be sorry that I know you. You're the most magnificent man I've ever met."

He laughed at that, half amused, half moved. And relieved, he discovered. The relief was tremendous. It made him laugh again. "Ryan, what an incredible thing to say."

She tilted up her chin. There would be no tears for him. "It's very true, but I won't tell you again. You'll get conceited." She lifted her palm to his cheek. "But just for tonight I'll let you enjoy it. And besides," she added, pulling his ear. "I like the way your eyebrows sweep up at the ends." She kissed his mouth, then let her lips roam his face. "And the way you write your name."

"The way I what?" he asked.

"On the contracts," Ryan elaborated, still planting light kisses all over his face. "It's very dashing." She felt the smile move his cheeks. "What do you like about me?" she demanded.

"Your taste," he said instantly. "It's impeccable."

Ryan bit his bottom lip, but he only rolled her over and turned the punishment into a very satisfying kiss. "I knew it would make you conceited," she said disgustedly. "I'm going to sleep."

"I don't think so," Pierce corrected, then lowered his mouth.

He was right again.

# Chapter Eleven

Saying good-bye to Pierce was one of the most difficult things Ryan had ever done. She had been tempted to forget every obligation, all of her ambitions, and ask him to take her with him. What were ambitions but empty goals if she was without him? She would tell him that she loved him, that nothing mattered but that they be together.

But when they had parted at the airport, she made herself smile, kiss him good-bye and let go. She had to drive into Los Angeles, and he had to drive up the coast. The work that had brought them together would also keep them apart.

There had still been no talk of the future. Ryan had come to learn that Pierce didn't speak of tomorrows. That he had spoken to her of his past, however briefly, reassured her. It was a step, perhaps a bigger one than either of them realized.

Time, Ryan thought, would tell if what had been between them in Las Vegas would strengthen or fade. This was the period of waiting. She knew that if he had regrets they would surface now while they were apart. Absence didn't always make the heart grow fonder. It also allowed the blood and the brain to cool. Doubts had a habit of forming when there was time to think. When he came to L.A. for the first meetings, she would have her answer.

When Ryan entered her office, she glanced at her watch and ruefully realized that time and schedules were part of her world again. She had left Pierce only an hour before and missed him unbearably already. Was he thinking of her—right now, at this moment? If she concentrated hard enough, would he know that she thought of him? With a sigh Ryan sat behind her desk. Since she had become involved with Pierce, she'd become freer with her imagination. There were times, she had to admit, that she believed in magic.

What's happened to you, Miss Swan? she asked herself. Your feet aren't on the ground, where they belong. Love, she mused and cupped her chin on her hands. When you're in love, nothing's impossible.

Who could say why her father had taken ill and sent her to Pierce? What force had guided her hand to choose that fateful card from the Tarot deck? Why had the cat picked her window in the storm? Certainly there were logical explanations for each step that had taken her closer to where she was at that moment. But a woman in love doesn't want logic.

It *had* been magic, Ryan thought with a smile. From the first moment their eyes had met, she had felt it. It had simply taken her time to accept it. Now that she did, her only choice was to wait and see if it lasted. No, she corrected, this wasn't a time for choices. She was going to make it last. If it took patience, then she'd be patient. If it took action, then she would act. But she was going to make it work, even if it meant trying her own hand at enchantment.

Shaking her head, she sat back in her chair. Nothing could be done until he was back in her life again. That would take a week. For now, there was still work to do. She couldn't wave a wand and brush the days away until he came back. She had to fill them. Flipping open her notes on Pierce Atkins, Ryan began to transcribe them. Less than thirty minutes later her buzzer sounded.

"Yes, Barbara."

"The boss wants you."

Ryan frowned at the litter of papers on her desk. "Now?"

"Now."

"All right, thanks." Swearing under her breath, Ryan stacked her papers, then separated what was in order to take with her. He might have given her a few hours to get organized, she thought. But the fact remained that he was going to be looking over her shoulder on this project. She was a long way from proving her worth to Bennett Swan. Knowing this, Ryan slipped papers into a folder and went to see her father.

"Good morning, Miss Swan." Bennett Swan's secretary glanced up as Ryan entered. "How was your trip?"

"It went very well, thank you." Ryan watched the woman's eyes shift briefly to the discreet, expensive pearl clusters at her ears. Ryan had worn her father's birthday gift knowing he would want to see them to assure himself they were correct and appreciated.

"Mr. Swan had to step out for a moment, but he'll be right with you. He'd like you to wait in his office. Mr. Ross is already inside."

"Welcome back, Ryan." Ned rose as she shut the door behind her. The coffee he held in his hand was steaming.

"Hello, Ned. Are you in on this meeting?"

"Mr. Swan wants me to work with you on this." He gave her a charming, half-apologetic smile. "Hope you don't mind."

"Of course not," she said flatly. Setting down the folder, she accepted the coffee Ned offered her. "In what capacity?"

"I'll be production coordinator," he told her. "It's still your baby, Ryan."

"Yes." With you as my proctor, she thought bitterly. Swan would still be calling the shots.

"How was Vegas?"

"Unique," Ryan told him as she wandered to the window.

"I hope you found some time to try your luck. You work too hard, Ryan."

She fingered the ankh at her neck and smiled. "I played some blackjack. I won."

"No kidding! Good for you."

After sipping at the coffee, she set the cup aside. "I think I have a firm basis for what will suit Pierce, Swan Productions and the network," she went on. "He doesn't need names to draw ratings. I think more than one guest star would crowd him. As for the set, I'll need to talk to the designers, but I have something fairly definite in mind already. As to the sponsors—"

"We can talk shop later," Ned interrupted. He moved to her and twined the ends of her hair around his fingers. Ryan stayed still and stared out of the window. "I've missed you, Ryan," Ned said softly. "It seemed as though you were gone for months."

"Strange," she murmured watching a plane cruise across the sky. "I've never known a week to pass so quickly."

"Darling, how long are you going to punish me?" He kissed the top of her head. Ryan felt no resentment. She felt nothing at all. Oddly, Ned had found himself more attracted to her since she had rejected him. There was something different about her now which he couldn't quite put his finger on. "If you'd just give me a chance, I could make it up to you."

"I'm not punishing you, Ned." Ryan turned to face him. "I'm sorry if it seems that way."

"You're still angry with me."

"No, I told you before that I wasn't." She sighed, deciding it would be better to clear the air between them. "I was angry and hurt, but it didn't last. I was never in love with you, Ned."

He didn't like the faint apology in her voice. It put him on the defensive. "We were just getting to know each other." When he started to take her hands, she shook her head.

"No, I don't think you know me at all. And," she added without rancor, "if we're going to be honest, that wasn't what you were after."

"Ryan, how many times do I have to apologize for that stupid suggestion?" There was a combination of hurt and regret in his voice.

"I'm not asking for an apology, Ned, I'm trying to make myself clear. You made a mistake assuming I could influence my father. You have more influence with him than I have."

"Ryan—"

"No, hear me out," she insisted. "You thought because I'm Bennett Swan's daughter I have his ear. That's just not true and never has been. His business associates have more input with him than I do. You wasted your time cultivating me to get to him. And, leaving that aside," she continued, "I'm not interested in a man who wants to use me as a springboard. I'm sure we'll work together very well, but I have no desire to see you outside of the office."

They both jolted when they heard the office door shut.

"Ryan...Ross." Bennett Swan walked over to his desk and sat down.

"Good morning." Ryan fumbled a bit over the greeting before she took a chair. How much had he heard? she wondered. His face revealed nothing, so Ryan reached for the folder. "I've outlined my thoughts and ideas on Atkins," she began, "though I haven't had time to complete a full report."

"Give me what you have." He waved Ned to a chair, then lit a cigar.

"He has a very tight club act." Ryan laced her fingers together to keep them still. "You've seen the tapes yourself, so you know that his act ranges from sleight of hand to large, complicated illusions to escapes that take two or three minutes. The escapes will keep him off camera for that amount of time, but the public expects that." She paused to cross her legs. "Of course, we know there'll have to be modifications for television, but I see no problem. He's an extraordinarily creative man."

Swan gave a grunt that might have been agreement and held out his hand for Ryan's report. Rising, she handed it to him, then took her seat again. He wasn't in one of his better moods, she noted. Someone had displeased him. She could only be grateful it hadn't been her.

"This is pretty slim," he commented, scowling at the folder.

"It won't be by the end of the day."

"I'll talk to Atkins myself next week," Swan stated as he skimmed through the papers. "Coogar's going to direct."

"Good, I'd like to work with him. I want Bloomfield on the set design," she said casually, then held her breath.

Swan glanced up and stared at her. Bloomfield had been his own choice. He'd decided on him less than an hour before. Ryan met the hard look unwaveringly. Swan wasn't altogether certain if he was pleased or annoyed that his daughter was one step ahead of him. "I'll consider it," he said and went back to her report. Quietly, Ryan let out her breath.

"He'll bring his own music director," she went on, thinking of Link. "And his own crew and gimmicks. If we have a problem, I'd say it'll be getting him to cooperate with our people in preproduction and on the set. He has his own way of doing things."

"That can be dealt with," Swan muttered. "Ross will be your production coordinator." Lifting his eyes, he met Ryan's.

"So I understand." Ryan met the look equally. "I can't argue with your choice, but I do feel that if I'm the producer on this project, I should pick my own team."

"You don't want to work with Ross?" Swan demanded as if Ned hadn't been sitting beside her.

"I think Ned and I will deal very well together," she said mildly. "And I'm sure Coogar knows the camera people he wants. It would be ridiculous to interfere with him. However," she added with a hint of steel in her voice, "I also know who *I* want working on this project."

Swan sat back and puffed for a moment on his cigar. The flush of color in his cheeks warned of temper. "What the hell do you know about producing?" he demanded.

"Enough to produce this special and make it a success," she replied. "Just as you told me to do a few weeks ago."

Swan had had time to regret the impulse that had made him agree to Pierce's terms. "You're the producer of record," he told her shortly. "Your name will be on the credits. Just do as you're told."

Ryan felt the tremor in her stomach but kept her eyes level. "If you feel that way, pull me now." She rose slowly. "But if I stay, I'm going to do more than watch my name roll on the credits. I know how this man works, and I know television. If that isn't enough for you, get someone else."

"Sit down!" he shouted at her. Ned sank a bit deeper in his own chair, but Ryan remained standing. "Don't give me ultimatums. I've been in this business for forty years." He banged his palm on the desk. "*Forty years!* So you know television," he said scornfully. "Pulling off a live show isn't like changing a damn contract. I can't have some hysterical little girl come running to me five minutes before air time telling me there's an equipment failure."

Ryan swallowed raw rage and answered coldly. "I'm not a hysterical little girl, and I've never come running to you for anything."

Completely stunned, he stared at her. The twinge of guilt made his anger all the more explosive. "You're just getting your feet wet," he snapped as he flipped the folder shut. "And you're getting them wet because

I say so. You're going to take my advice when I give it to you."

"Your advice?" Ryan countered. Her eyes glistened with conflicting emotions, but her voice was very firm. "I've always respected your advice, but I haven't heard any here today. Just orders. I don't want any favors from you." She turned and headed for the door.

"Ryan!" There was absolute fury in the word. No one but no one walked out on Bennett Swan. "Come back here and sit down. *Young lady!*" he bellowed when she ignored the command.

"I'm not your young lady," she returned, spinning back. "I'm your employee."

Taken aback, he stared at her. What answer could he make to that? He waved his hand at a chair impatiently. "Sit down," he said again, but she stayed at the door. "Sit, sit," he repeated with more exasperation than temper.

Ryan came back and calmly took her place.

"Take Ryan's notes and start working on budget," he told Ned.

"Yes, sir." Grateful for the dismissal, Ned took the folder and retreated. Swan waited for the door to close before he looked back at his daughter.

"What do you want?" he asked her for the first time in his life. The fact occurred to them both at the same moment.

Ryan took time to separate her personal and professional feelings. "The same respect you'd show any other producer."

"You haven't got any track record," he pointed out.

"No," she agreed. "And I never will if you tie my hands."

Swan let out a sigh, saw his cigar was dead and dropped it in an ashtray. "The network has a tentative slot, the third Sunday in May, nine to ten east coast time."

"That only gives us two months."

He nodded. "They want it before the summer season. How fast can you work?"

Ryan lifted a brow and smiled. "Fast enough. I want Elaine Fisher to guest star."

Swan narrowed his eyes at her. "Is that all?" he asked dryly.

"No, but it's a start. She's talented, beautiful and as popular with women as she is with men. Plus, she's had experience at working clubs and live theater," she pointed out as Swan frowned and said nothing. "That guileless, wide-eyed look of hers is the perfect contrast for Pierce."

"She's shooting in Chicago."

"That film wraps next week." Ryan sent him a calm smile. "And she's under contract with Swan. If the film goes a week or two over schedule, it won't matter," she added as he remained silent. "We won't need her in California for more than a few days. Pierce carries the show."

"She has other commitments," Swan pointed out.

"She'll fit it in."

"Call her agent."

"I will." Ryan rose again. "I'll set up a meeting with Coogar and get back to you." She paused a moment, then on impulse walked around his desk to stand beside his chair. "I've watched you work for years," she began. "I don't expect you to have the confidence in me you have in yourself or someone with experience. And if I make mistakes, I wouldn't want them to be overlooked. But if I do a good job, and I'm going to, I want to be sure *I* did it, not that I just got the credit for it."

"Your show," he said simply.

"Yes." Ryan nodded. "Exactly. There are a lot of reasons why this project is particularly important to me. I can't promise not to make mistakes, but I can promise you there's no one else who'll work harder on it."

"Don't let Coogar push you around," he muttered after a moment. "He likes to drive producers crazy."

Ryan smiled. "I've heard the stories, don't worry." She started to leave again, then remembered. After a brief hesitation, she leaned down to brush his cheek with her lips. "Thank you for the earrings. They're lovely."

Swan glanced at them. The jeweler had assured his secretary they were an appropriate gift and a good investment. What had he said in the note he had sent with them? he wondered. Chagrined that he couldn't remember, he decided to ask his secretary for a copy of it.

"Ryan." Swan took her hand. Seeing her blink in surprise at the gesture, he stared down at his own fingers. He had heard all of her conversation with Ned before he had come into the office. It had angered him, disturbed him, and now, when he saw his daughter stunned that he took her hand, it left him frustrated.

"Did you have a good time in Vegas?" he asked, not knowing what else to say.

"Yes." Uncertain what to do next, Ryan went back to business. "I think it was a smart move. Watching Pierce work up close gave me a good perspective. It's a much more overall view than a tape. And I got to know the people who work with him. That won't hurt when they have to work with me." She gave their joined hands another confused look. Could he be ill? she wondered and glanced quickly at his face. "I'll— I'll have a much more concise report for you by tomorrow."

Swan waited until she was finished. "Ryan, how old were you yesterday?" He watched her closely. Her eyes went from bewildered to bleak.

"Twenty-seven," she told him flatly.

*Twenty-seven!* On a long breath, Swan released her hand. "I've lost some years somewhere," he mumbled. "Go set up with Coogar," he told her and shuffled through the papers on his desk. "Send me a memo after you contact Fisher's agent."

"All right."

Over the top of the papers, Swan watched her walk to the door. When she had left him, he sat back in his chair. He found it staggering to realize he was getting old.

# Chapter Twelve

Producing, Ryan found, kept her as effectively buried in paper work as contracts had. She spent her days behind her desk, on the phone or in someone else's office. It was hard, grueling work with little glamour. The hours were long, the problems endless. Yet she found she had a taste for it. She was, after all, her father's daughter.

Swan hadn't given her a free hand, but their confrontation on the morning of her return to L.A. had had its benefits. He was listening to her. For the most part she found him surprisingly agreeable to her proposals. He didn't veto arbitrarily as she had feared he would but altered from time to time. Swan knew the business from every angle. Ryan listened and learned.

Her days were full and chaotic. Her nights were empty. Ryan had known Pierce wouldn't phone her. It wasn't his way. He would be down in his workroom, planning, practicing, perfecting. She doubted he would even notice the passing of time.

Of course, she could phone him, Ryan thought as she wandered around her empty apartment. She could invent any number of viable excuses for calling him. There was the change in the taping schedule. That was a valid reason, though she knew he'd already been informed through his agent. And there were at least a dozen minor points they could go over before the meeting the following week.

Ryan glanced thoughtfully at the phone, then shook her head. It wasn't business that she wanted to discuss with him, and she wouldn't use it as a smoke screen. Going into the kitchen, she began to prepare herself a light supper.

Pierce ran through the water illusion for a third time. It was nearly perfect. But nearly was never good enough. He thought, not for the first time, that the camera's eye would be infinitely sharper than the human eye. Every time he had watched himself on tape, he had found flaws. It didn't matter to Pierce that only he knew where to look for them. It only mattered that they were there. He ran through the illusion again.

His workroom was quiet. Though he knew Link was upstairs at the piano, the sound didn't carry down to him. But he wouldn't have heard it if they had been in the same room. Critically, he watched himself in a long mirror as water seemed to shimmer in an unsupported tube. The mirror showed him holding it, top and bottom, while it flowed from palm to palm. Water. It was only one of the four elements he intended to command for Ryan's special.

He thought of the special as hers more than his own. He thought of her when he should have been thinking of his work. With a graceful movement of his hands, Pierce had the water pouring back into a glass pitcher.

He had almost phoned her a dozen times. Once, at three o'clock in the morning, his hand had been on the dial. Just her voice—he had only wanted to hear her voice. He hadn't completed the call, reminding himself of his vow never to put obligations on anyone. If he phoned, it meant he expected her to be there to answer. Ryan was free to do as she pleased; he had no claim on her. Or on anyone. Even the bird he kept had its cage door open at all times.

There had been no one in his life whom he had belonged to. Social workers had brought rules and compassion, but ultimately he had been just one more name in the file. The law had seen to it that he was properly placed and properly cared for. And the law had kept him bound to two people who didn't want him but wouldn't set him free.

Even when he loved—as with Link and Bess—he accepted but demanded no bonds. Perhaps that was why he continued to devise more complicated escapes. Each time he succeeded, it proved no one could be held forever.

Yet he thought of Ryan when he should have been working.

Picking up the handcuffs, Pierce studied them. They had fit cleanly over her wrist. He had held her then. Idly, he snapped one half over his right wrist and toyed with the other, imagining Ryan's hand locked to his.

Was that what he wanted? he wondered. To lock her to him? He remembered how warm she was, how steeped in her he would become after one touch. Who would be locked to whom? Annoyed, Pierce released himself as swiftly as he had snapped on the cuff.

"Double, double, toil and trouble," Merlin croaked from his perch.

Amused, Pierce glanced over. "I think you're quite right," he murmured, jiggling the cuffs in his hand a moment. "But then, you couldn't resist her either, could you?"

"Abracadabra."

"Abracadabra indeed," Pierce agreed absently. "But who's bewitched whom?"

Ryan was just about to step into the tub when she heard the knock on the door. "Damn!" Irritated by the interruption, she slipped back into her robe and went to answer. Even as she pulled the door open, she was calculating how to get rid of the visitor before her bath water chilled.

"Pierce!"

He saw her eyes widen in surprise. Then, with a mixture of relief and pleasure, he saw the joy. Ryan launched herself into his arms.

"Are you real?" she demanded before her mouth fastened on his. Her hunger shot through him, matching his own. "Five days," Ryan murmured and clung to him. "Do you know how many hours there are in five days?"

"A hundred and twenty." Pierce drew her away to smile at her. "We'd better go inside. Your neighbors are finding this very entertaining."

Ryan pulled him in and shut the door by pressing him back against it. "Kiss me," she demanded. "Hard. Hard enough for a hundred and twenty hours."

His mouth came down on hers. She felt the scrape of his teeth against her lips as he groaned and crushed her to him. Pierce struggled to remember his strength and her fragility, but her tongue was probing, her hands were seeking. She was laughing that husky, aroused laugh that drove him wild.

"Oh, you're real." Ryan sighed and rested her head on his shoulder. "You're real."

But are you? he wondered, a little dazed by the kiss.

After one last hug she pulled out of his arms. "What are you doing here, Pierce? I didn't expect you until Monday or Tuesday."

"I wanted to see you," he said simply and lifted his palm to her cheek. "To touch you."

Ryan caught his hand and pressed the palm to her lips. A fire kindled in the pit of his stomach. "I've missed you," she murmured as her eyes clung to his. "So much. If I had known wishing you here would bring you, I'd have wished harder."

"I wasn't certain you'd be free."

"Pierce," she said softly and laid her hands on his chest. "Do you really think I want to be with anyone else?"

He stared down at her without speaking, but she felt the increased rate of his heartbeat under her hand. "You interfere with my work," he said at length.

Puzzled, Ryan tilted her head. "I do? How?"

"You're in my mind when you shouldn't be."

"I'm sorry." But she smiled, clearly showing she wasn't. "I've been breaking your concentration?"

"Yes."

She slid her hands up to his neck. "That's too bad." Her voice was mocking and seductive. "What are you going to do about it?"

For an answer, Pierce dragged her to the floor. The movement was so swift, so unexpected, Ryan gasped but the sound was swallowed by his mouth. The robe was whipped from her before she could draw a breath. Pierce took her to the summit so quickly, she was powerless to do anything but answer the desperate mutual need.

His clothes were gone with more speed than was reasonable, but he gave her no time to explore him. In one move Pierce rolled her on top of him, then, lifting her as though she were weightless, he set her down to plunge fully inside her.

Ryan cried out, stunned, exhilarated. The speed had her mind spinning. The heat had her skin drenched. Her eyes grew wide as pleasure went beyond all possibilities. She could see Pierce's face, damp with passion, eyes closed. She could hear each tearing breath as he dug his long fingers into her hips to keep her moving with him. Then a film was over her eyes—a white, misty film that hazed her vision. She pressed her hands to his chest to keep from falling. But she was falling, slowly, slowly, drained of everything.

When the mist cleared, Ryan found she was in his arms with his face buried in her hair. Their damp bodies were fused together.

"Now I know you're real, too," Pierce murmured and helped himself to her mouth. "How do you feel?"

"Dazed," Ryan answered breathlessly. "Wonderful."

Pierce laughed. Rising, he lifted her into his arms. "I'm going to take you to bed and love you again before you recover."

"*Mmm,* yes." Ryan nuzzled his neck. "I should let the water out of the tub first."

Pierce lifted a brow, then smiled. With Ryan half-dozing in his arms, he wandered the apartment until he found the bath. "Were you in the tub when I knocked?"

"Almost." Ryan sighed and snuggled against him. "I was going to get rid of whoever had interrupted me. I was very annoyed."

With a flick of his wrist, Pierce turned the hot water on full. "I didn't notice."

"Couldn't you see how I was trying to get rid of you?"

"I have very thick skin at times," he confessed. "I suppose the water's cooled off a bit by now."

"Probably," she agreed.

"You use a free hand with the bubbles."

"*Mmm-hmm.* Oh!" Ryan's eyes shot open as she found herself lowered into the tub.

"Cold?" He grinned at her.

"No." Ryan reached up and turned off the water that steamed hot into the tub. For a moment she allowed her eyes to feast on him—the long, lean body, the wiry muscles and narrow hips. She tilted her head and twirled a finger in the bubbles. "Would you like to join me?" she invited politely.

"The thought had crossed my mind."

"Please." She gestured with her hand. "Be my guest. I've been very rude. I didn't even offer you a drink." She gave him a sassy grin.

The water rose when Pierce lowered himself into it. He sat at the foot of the tub, facing her. "I don't often drink," he reminded her.

"Yes, I know." She gave him a sober nod. "You don't smoke, rarely drink, hardly ever swear. You're a paragon of virtue, Mr. Atkins."

He threw a handful of bubbles at her.

"In any case," Ryan continued, brushing them from her cheek, "I did want to discuss the sketches for the set design with you. Would you like the soap?"

"Thank you, Miss Swan." He took it from her. "You were going to tell me about the set?"

"Oh, yes, I think you'll approve the sketches, though you might want some minor changes." She shifted, sighing a little as her legs brushed against his.

"I told Bloomfield I wanted something a little fanciful, medieval, but not too cluttered."

"No suits of armor?"

"No, just atmosphere. Something moody, like..." She broke off when he took her foot in his hand and began to soap it.

"Yes?" he prompted.

"A tone," she said as gentle pulses of pleasure ran up her leg. "Muted colors. The sort you have in your parlor."

Pierce began to massage her calf. "Only one set?"

Ryan trembled in the steamy water as he slid soapy fingers up her leg. "Yes, I thought—*mmm*—I thought the basic mood..." He moved his hands slowly up and down her legs as he watched her face.

"What mood?" He lifted a hand to soap her breast in circles while using his other to massage the top of her thigh.

"Sex," Ryan breathed. "You're very sexy onstage."

"Am I?" Through drugging ripples of sensation, she heard the amusement in the question.

"Yes, dramatic and rather coolly sexy. When I watch you perform..." She trailed off, struggling for breath. The heady scent of the bath salts rose around her. She felt the water lap under her breasts, just below Pierce's clever hand. "Your hands," she managed, steeped in hot, tortured pleasure.

"What about them?" he asked as he slipped a finger inside her.

"Magic." The word trembled out. "Pierce, I can't talk when you're doing things to me."

"Shall I stop?" She was no longer looking at him. Her eyes were closed, but he watched her face, using fingertips only to arouse her.

"No." Ryan found his hand under the water and pressed it against herself.

"You're so beautiful, Ryan." The water swayed as he moved to nibble at her breast, then at her mouth. "So soft. I could see you when I was alone in the middle of the night. I could imagine touching you like this. I couldn't stay away."

"Don't." Her hands were in his hair, pulling his mouth more firmly to hers. "Don't stay away. I've waited so long already."

"Five days," he murmured as he urged her legs apart.

"All my life."

At her words something coursed through him which passion wouldn't permit him to explore. He had to have her, that was all.

"Pierce," Ryan murmured hazily. "We're going to sink."

"Hold your breath," he suggested and took her.


"I'm sure my father will want to see you," Ryan told Pierce the next morning as he pulled into her space in the parking complex of Swan Productions. "And I imagine you'd like to see Coogar."

"Since I'm here," Pierce agreed and shut off the ignition. "But I came to see you."

With a smile Ryan leaned over and kissed him. "I'm so glad you did. Can you stay over the weekend, or do you have to get back?"

He tucked a lock of hair behind her ear. "We'll see."

She slid from the car. She could hope for no better answer. "Of course, the first full meeting isn't scheduled until next week, but I imagine they'll accommodate you." They walked into the building. "I can make the calls from my office."

Ryan led him down the corridors briskly, nodding or answering now and again when someone greeted her. She was all business, he noted, the moment she stepped through the front doors.

"I don't know where Bloomfield is today," she continued as she pushed the button in the elevator for her floor. "But if he's unavailable, I can get the sketches and go over them with you myself." They stepped inside as she began to outline her day's schedule, balancing and altering to allow for Pierce's presence. "You and I might go over the timing, too," she continued. "We have fifty-two minutes to fill. And..."

"Will you have dinner with me tonight, Miss Swan?"

Ryan broke off what she was saying and found him smiling at her. The look in his eyes made it difficult for her to recall her plans for the day. She could only remember what had passed in the night. "I think I might fit that into my schedule, Mr. Atkins," she murmured as the elevator doors opened.

"You'll check your calendar?" he asked and kissed her hand.

"Yes." Ryan had to stop the doors from closing again. "And don't look at me like that today," she said breathlessly. "I'll never be able to function."

"Is that so?" Pierce let her pull him into the corridor. "I might consider it suitable revenge for all the times you've made it impossible for me to do my work."

Unnerved, Ryan led him into her office. "If we're going to manage to pull off this show..." she began.

"Oh, I have complete faith in the very organized, very dependable Miss Swan," Pierce said easily. He took a chair and waited for her to sit behind her desk.

"You're going to be difficult to work with, aren't you?" she asked.

"Most likely."

Wrinkling her nose at him, Ryan picked up the phone and pushed a series of buttons. "Ryan Swan," she announced, deliberately keeping her eyes away from Pierce. "Is he free?"

"Please hold, Miss Swan."

In a moment she heard her father's voice answer impatiently. "Make it fast, I'm busy."

"I'm sorry to disturb you," she said automatically. "I have Pierce Atkins in my office. I thought you might like to see him."

"What's he doing here?" Swan demanded, then continued before Ryan could answer. "Bring him up." He hung up without waiting for her agreement.

"He'd like to see you now," Ryan said as she replaced the receiver.

Pierce nodded, rising as she did. The brevity of the phone conversation had told him a great deal. Minutes later, after entering Swan's office, he learned a great deal more.

"Mr. Atkins." Swan rose to come around his massive desk with his hand extended. "What a pleasant surprise. I didn't expect to meet you personally until next week."

"Mr. Swan." Pierce accepted the offered hand and noted Swan had no greeting for his daughter.

"Please sit down," he suggested with a wide sweep of his hand. "What can I get for you? Coffee?"

"No, nothing."

"Swan Productions is very pleased to have your talents, Mr. Atkins." Swan settled behind his desk again. "We're going to put a lot of energy into this special. Promotion and press have already been set into motion."

"So I understand. Ryan keeps me informed."

"Of course." Swan sent her a quick nod. "We'll shoot in studio twenty-five. Ryan can arrange for you to see it today if you'd like. And anything else you'd like to see while you're here." He sent her another look.

"Yes, of course," she answered. "I thought Mr. Atkins might like to see Coogar and Bloomfield if they're available."

"Set it up," he ordered, dismissing her. "Now, Mr. Atkins, I have a letter from your representative. There are a few points we might go over before you meet the more artistic members of the company."

Pierce waited until Ryan had shut the door behind her. "I intend to work with Ryan, Mr. Swan. I contracted with you with that stipulation."

"Naturally," Swan answered, thrown off balance. As a rule talent was flattered to receive his personal attention. "I can assure you she's been hard at work on your behalf."

"I don't doubt it."

Swan met the measuring gray eyes levelly. "Ryan is producing your special at your request."

"Your daughter is a very interesting woman, Mr. Swan." Pierce waited a moment, watching Swan's eyes narrow. "On a professional level," he continued smoothly. "I have complete faith in her abilities. She's sharp and observant and very serious about her business."

"I'm delighted you're satisfied with her," Swan replied, not certain what lay beyond Pierce's words.

"It would be a remarkably stupid man who wasn't satisfied with her," Pierce countered, then continued before Swan could react. "Don't you find talent and professionalism pleasing, Mr. Swan?"

Swan studied Pierce a moment, then leaned back in his chair. "I wouldn't be the head of Swan Productions if I didn't," he said wryly.

"Then we understand each other," Pierce said mildly. "Just what are the points you would like to clear up?"

It was five-fifteen before Ryan was able to wind up the meeting with Bloomfield and Pierce. She'd been on the run all day, arranging spur-of-the-moment conferences and covering her scheduled work. There had been no moment to spare for a *tête-à-tête* with Pierce. Now, as they walked down the corridor together from Bloomfield's office, she let out a long breath.

"Well, that seems to be about it. Nothing like the unexpected appearance of a magician to throw everybody into a dither. As seasoned as Bloomfield is, I think he was just waiting for you to pull a rabbit out of your hat."

"I didn't have a hat," Pierce pointed out.

"Would that stop you?" Ryan laughed and checked her watch. "I'll have to stop by my office and clear up a couple of things, touch base with my father and let him know the talent was properly fussed over, then..."

"No."

"No?" Ryan looked up in surprise. "Is there something else you wanted to see? Was there something wrong with the sketches?"

"No," Pierce said again. "You're not going back to your office to clear up a couple of things or to touch base with your father."

Ryan laughed again and continued to walk. "It won't take long, twenty minutes."

"You agreed to have dinner with me, Miss Swan," he reminded her.

"As soon as I clear my desk."

"You can clear your desk Monday morning. Is there something urgent?"

"Well, no, but..." She trailed off when she felt something on her wrist, then stared down at the handcuff. "Pierce, what are you doing?" Ryan tugged her arm but found it firmly chained to his.

"Taking you to dinner."

"Pierce, take this thing off," she ordered with amused exasperation. "It's ridiculous."

"Later," he promised before he pulled her to the elevator. He waited calmly for it to reach their floor as two secretaries eyed him, the cuffs and Ryan.

"Pierce," she said in undertones. "Take these off right now. They're staring at us."

"Who?"

"Pierce, I mean it!" She let out a frustrated moan as the doors opened and revealed several other members of Swan Productions' staff. Pierce stepped inside the car, leaving her no choice but to follow. "You're going to pay for this," she muttered, trying to ignore speculative stares.

"Tell me, Miss Swan," Pierce said in a friendly, carrying voice, "is it always so difficult to persuade you to keep a dinner engagement?"

After an unintelligible mutter, Ryan stared straight ahead.

Still handcuffed to Pierce, Ryan walked across the parking lot. "All right, joke's over," she insisted. "Take these off. I've never been so embarrassed in my life! Do you have any idea how—"

But her heated lecture was cut off by his mouth. "I've wanted to do that all day," Pierce told her, then kissed her again before she could retort.

Ryan tried her best to hang onto her annoyance. His mouth was so soft. His hand, as it pressed into the small of her back, was so gentle. She drew closer to him, but when she started to lift her arms around his neck, the handcuff prevented her. "No," she said firmly, remembering. "You're not going to sneak out of this one." Ryan pulled away, ready to rage at him. He smiled at her. "Damn you, Pierce," she said on a sigh. "Kiss me again."

He kissed her softly. "You're very exciting when you're angry, Miss Swan," he whispered.

"I *was* angry," she muttered, kissing him back. "I *am* angry."

"And exciting." He drew her over to the car.

"Well?" Holding their joined wrists aloft, she sent him an inquiring glance. Pierce opened the car door and gestured her inside. "Pierce!" Exasperated, Ryan jiggled her arm. "Take these off. You can't drive this way."

"Of course I can. You'll have to climb over," he instructed, nudging her into the car.

Ryan sat in the driver's seat a moment and glared at him. "This is absurd."

"Yes," he agreed. "And I'm enjoying it. Move over."

Ryan considered refusing but decided he would simply lift her into the passenger seat bodily. With little trouble and less grace, she managed it. Pierce gave her another smile as he switched on the ignition.

"Put your hand on the gearshift and we'll do very well."

Ryan obeyed. His palm rested on the back of her hand as he put the car in reverse. "Just how long are you going to leave these on?"

"Interesting question. I haven't decided." He pulled out of the parking lot and headed north.

Ryan shook her head, then laughed in spite of herself. "If you'd told me you were this hungry, I'd have come along peacefully."

"I'm not hungry," he said easily. "I thought we'd stop and eat on the way."

"On the way?" Ryan repeated. "On the way where?"

"Home."

"Home?" A glance out the window showed her he was heading out of L.A. in the opposite direction of her apartment. "*Your* home?" she asked incredulously. "Pierce, that's a hundred and fifty miles from here."

"More or less," he agreed. "You're not needed in L.A. until Monday."

"Monday! Do you mean we're going there for the weekend? But I can't." She hadn't thought she could be any more exasperated than she already was. "I can't just pop in the car and go off for a weekend."

"Why not?"

"Well, I..." He made it sound so reasonable, she had to search for the flaw. "Because I can't. I don't have any clothes, for one thing, and—"

"You won't need them."

That stopped her. Ryan stared at him while a strange mixture of excitement and panic ran through her. "I think you're kidnapping me."

"Exactly."

"Oh."

"Any objections?" he asked, giving her a brief glance.

"I'll let you know Monday," she told him and settled back in the seat, prepared to enjoy her abduction.

# Chapter Thirteen

Ryan awoke in Pierce's bed. She opened her eyes to streaming sunlight. It had barely been dawn when Pierce had awakened her to murmur that he was going down to work. Ryan reached for his pillow, drew it closer and lingered a few minutes longer in bed.

What a surprising man he was, she mused. She would never have thought he would do anything as outrageous as handcuffing her to him and bundling her off for a weekend with nothing more than the clothes on her back. She should have been angry, indignant.

Ryan buried her face in his pillow. How could she be? Could you be angry with a man for showing you—with a look, with a touch—that you were needed and desired? Could you be indignant when a man wanted you enough to spirit you off to make love to you as though you were the most precious creature on earth?

Ryan stretched luxuriously, then picked up her watch from the nightstand. Nine-thirty! she thought with a jolt. How could it be so late? It seemed only moments ago that Pierce had left her. Jumping from the bed, she raced to the shower. They only had two days together; she wasn't going to waste them sleeping.

When she came back into the bedroom with a towel wrapped around her, Ryan studied her clothes dubiously. There was something to be said for being kidnapped by a dashing magician, she admitted, but it was really too bad he hadn't let her **pack** something first. Philosophically, she began to dress in the suit she had worn the day before. He'd simply have to find her something else to wear, she decided, but for now she'd make do.

With some consternation Ryan realized she didn't even have her purse with her. It was still in the bottom drawer of her desk. She wrinkled her nose at the reflection in the mirror. Her hair was tumbled, her face naked of cosmetics. Not even a comb and a lipstick, she thought and sighed. Pierce was going to have to conjure up something. With this in mind she went downstairs to look for him.

When she came to the foot of the stairs, she saw Link getting ready to leave. "Good morning." Ryan hesitated, unsure what to say to him. He'd been nowhere to be seen when they had arrived the night before.

"Hi." He grinned at her. "Pierce said you were here."

"Yes, I—he invited me for the weekend." It seemed the simplest way to put it.

"I'm glad you came. He missed you."

Her eyes lit up at that. "I missed him, too. Is he here?"

"In the library. He's on the phone." He hesitated, and Ryan saw the faint pink flush in his cheeks.

Smiling, she came down the last step. "What is it, Link?"

"I—uh—I finished writing that song you liked."

"That's wonderful. I'd love to hear it."

"It's on the piano." Excruciatingly embarrassed, he lowered his eyes to his shoes. "You can play it later if you want to."

"Won't you be here?" She wanted to take his hand as she would a little boy's but felt it would only embarrass him more. "I've never heard you play."

"No, I'm..." His color deepened, and he sent her a quick look. "Bess and I...well, she wanted to drive to San Francisco." He cleared his throat. "She likes to ride the streetcars."

"That's nice, Link." On impulse, Ryan decided to see if she could give Bess a hand. "She's a very special lady, isn't she?"

"Oh, sure. There's nobody else like Bess," he agreed readily, then stared at his shoes again.

"She feels just the same way about you."

His eyes darted to her face, then over her shoulder. "You think so?"

"Oh, yes." Though she wanted badly to smile, Ryan kept her voice serious. "She told me how she first met you. I thought it was terribly romantic."

Link gave a nervous little laugh. "She was awful pretty. Lots of guys hang around her when we go on the road."

"I imagine so," Ryan agreed and gave him a mental shove. "But I think she has a taste for musicians. Piano players," she added when he looked back at her. "The kind who know how to write beautifully romantic songs. Time's wasting, don't you think?"

Link was staring at her as though trying to sort out her words. "Huh? Oh, yeah." He wrinkled his brow, then nodded. "Yeah, I guess so. I should go get her now."

"I think that's a very good idea." She did take his hand now, giving it a quick squeeze. "Have a good time."

"Okay." He smiled and turned for the door. With his hand on the knob, he stopped to look over his shoulder. "Ryan, does she really like piano players?"

"Yes, Link, she really does."

He grinned again and opened the door. "Bye."

"Goodbye, Link. Give Bess my love."

When the door shut, Ryan remained where she was a moment. What a sweet man, she thought, then crossed her fingers for Bess. They would be wonderful together if they could just get over the obstacle of his shyness. Well, Ryan thought with a pleased smile, she had certainly done all she could in her first attempt at matchmaking. The rest was **up** to the two of them.

Turning down the hall, she went to the library. The door was open, and she could hear Pierce's low-pitched voice as it carried to her. Even the sound of it had something stirring inside her. He was here with her, and they were alone. When she stood in the doorway, his eyes met hers.

Pierce smiled, and continued his conversation, gestured her inside. "I'll send you the exact specifications in writing," he said, watching Ryan enter and wander to a bookshelf. Why was it, he wondered, that the sight of her in one of those prim business suits never failed to excite him? "No, I'll need it completed in three weeks. I can't give you any more time than that," he continued with his eyes fixed on Ryan's back. "I need time to work with it before I can be sure I can use it."

Ryan turned around, then, perching on the arm of a chair, she watched him. He wore jeans with a short-sleeved sweatshirt, and his hair was disheveled, as though he had run his hands through it. She thought he had never looked more attractive, sunk back in an overstuffed chair, more relaxed than usual. The energy was still there, the live-wire energy that seemed to spark from him onstage or off. But it was on hold, she mused. He was more at ease in this house than he was anywhere else.

He continued to give instructions to whomever it was he spoke to, but Ryan watched his eyes skim her briefly. Something impish shot through her. Perhaps she could ruffle that calm of his.

Rising idly, she began to wander the room again, stepping out of her shoes as she did so. She took a book from the shelf, skimmed through it, then replaced it.

"I'll need the entire list delivered here," Pierce stated and watched Ryan slip out of her suit jacket. She draped it over the back of a chair. "Yes, that's exactly what I want. If you'll—" He broke off as she began to unbutton her blouse. She looked up when he stopped speaking and smiled at him. "If you'll contact me when you have..." The blouse slid to the floor before she casually unzipped her skirt. "When you have..." Pierce went on, struggling to remember what he had been saying, "the—ah—all the items, I'll arrange for the freight."

Bending over after she stepped out of her skirt, Ryan began to unhook her stockings. "No, that won't—it won't be necessary." She tossed her hair behind her shoulder and sent Pierce another smile. The look held for several pulsing seconds. "Yes," Pierce mumbled into the phone. "Yes, that's fine."

Leaving the pool of nylons on the discarded skirt, she straightened. Her chemise laced up the front. With one finger Ryan pulled at the small bow between her breasts until it loosened. She kept her eyes on his, smiling again when she watched them lower to where her fingers worked slowly with the laces.

"What?" Pierce shook his head. The man's voice had been nothing but an unintelligible buzz in his ear. "What?" he said again as the silk parted. Very slowly, Ryan drew it off. "I'll get back to you." Pierce dropped the receiver back on the hook.

"All finished?" she asked as she walked to him. "I wanted to talk to you about my wardrobe."

"I like what you have on." He pulled her into the chair with him and found her mouth. Tasting the wild need, she let herself go limp.

"Was that an important call?" she asked when his lips moved to her neck. "I didn't want to disturb you."

"The hell you didn't." He reached for her breast, groaning when he took possession. "God, you drive me crazy! Ryan . . ." His voice was rough with urgency as he slid her to the floor. "Now."

"Yes," she murmured even as he entered her.

He trembled as he lay on top of her. His breath was ragged. No one, he thought, no one had ever been able to destroy his control this way. It was terrifying. Part of him wanted to stand up and walk away—to prove he could still walk away. But he stayed where he was.

"Dangerous," he murmured in her ear just before he let the tip of his tongue trace it. He heard her sigh. "You're a dangerous woman."

"*Mmm,* how so?"

"You know my weaknesses, Ryan Swan. Maybe you are my weakness."

"Is that bad?" she murmured.

"I don't know." He lifted his head and stared down at her. "I don't know."

Ryan lifted a hand to tenderly brush the hair from his forehead. "It doesn't matter today. Today there's only the two of us."

The look he gave her was long and deep, as intense as the first time their eyes had met. "The more I'm with you, the more there are only the two of us."

She smiled, then pulled him back to cradle him in her arms. "The first time you kissed me, the whole world dropped away. I tried to tell myself you had hypnotized me."

Pierce laughed and reached up to fondle her breast. The nipple was still taut, and she quivered at his touch. "Do you have any idea how badly I wanted to take you to bed that night?" He ran his thumb lazily back and forth over the point of her breast, listening to her quickening breathing as he spoke. "I couldn't work, I couldn't sleep. I lay there thinking about how you'd looked in that little bit of silk and lace."

"I wanted you," Ryan said huskily as fresh passion kindled. "I was shocked that I'd only known you for a few hours and I wanted you."

"I would have made love to you like this that night." Pierce touched his mouth to hers. He kissed her, using his lips only until hers were hot and soft and hungry. Both of his hands were in her hair now, drawing it back from her face as his tongue gently plundered.

It seemed he would kiss her endlessly. There were soft, murmuring sounds as their lips parted and met again, then again. Hot, heady, unbearably sweet. He stroked her shoulders, lingering at the slope while the kiss went on and on. She knew the world centered on his lips.

No matter where else he touched, his mouth remained on hers. He might run his hands wherever he chose, but his kiss alone kept her prisoner. He seemed to crave her taste more than he craved breath. She gripped his shoulders, digging her nails into his flesh and totally unaware of it. Her only thought was that the kiss go on forever.

He knew her body was totally his and touched where it gave them both the most pleasure. At the slightest urging, her legs parted for him. He traced a fingertip up and down the inside of her thigh, delighting in its silken texture and in her trembling response. He passed over the center of her only briefly on the journey to her other thigh, all the while toying with her lips.

He used his teeth and his tongue, then his lips only. Her delirious murmuring of his name sent fresh thrills racing along his skin. There was the subtle sweep of her hips to trace, the curve of her waist. Her arms were satin smooth. He could find endless delight in touching only them. She was his—he thought it again and had to control an explosive urge to take her quickly. Instead, he let the kiss speak for him. It spoke of dark, driving needs and infinite tenderness.

Even when he slipped inside her, Pierce continued to savor the taste of her mouth. He took her slowly, waiting for her needs to build, forcing back his own passion until it was no longer possible to deny it.

His mouth was still crushed to hers when she cried out with the final flash of pleasure.

No one but her, he thought dizzily as he breathed in the scent of her hair. No one but her. Ryan's arms came around him to keep him close. He knew he was trapped.

Hours later Ryan slid two steaks under the broiler. She was dressed now in a pair of Pierce's jeans, cinched at the waist with a belt, with the legs rolled up several times to adjust for their difference in height. The sweatshirt bagged over her hips. Ryan pushed the sleeves up past the elbow while she helped him prepare dinner.

"Do you cook as well as Link?" she demanded, turning to watch him add croutons to the salad he was making.

"No. When you're kidnapped, Miss Swan, you can't expect gourmet meals."

Ryan went to stand behind him, then slipped her arms around his waist. "Are you going to demand a ransom?" With a sigh she rested her cheek on his back. She had never been happier in her life.

"Perhaps. When I'm through with you."

She pinched him hard, but he didn't even flinch. "Louse," she said lovingly, then slipped her hands under his shirt to trail her fingers up his chest. This time she felt him quiver.

"You distract me, Ryan."

"I was hoping to. It isn't the simplest thing to do, you know."

"You've been having a remarkable streak of success," he commented as she ran her hands over his shoulders.

"Can you really dislocate your shoulders to get out of a straightjacket?" she wondered aloud as she felt the strength of their solidity.

Amused, he continued to cube cheese for the salad. "Where did you hear that?"

"Oh, somewhere," she said vaguely, not willing to admit she had devoured every write-up she could find on him. "I also heard you have complete control over your muscles." They rippled under her curious fingers. She pressed into his back, enjoying the faint forest scent that clung to him.

"Do you also hear that I only eat certain herbs and roots that I gather under a full moon?" He popped a morsel of cheese in his mouth before he turned to gather her into his arms. "Or that I studied the magic arts in Tibet when I was twelve?"

"I read that you were tutored by Houdini's ghost," she countered.

"Really? I must have missed that one. Very flattering."

"You really enjoy the ridiculous things they print about you, don't you?"

"Of course." He kissed her nose. "I'd have a sorry sense of humor if I didn't."

"And of course," she added, "if the fact and fantasy are so mixed, nobody ever knows which is which or who you are."

"There's that, too." He twined a lock of her hair around his finger. "The more they print about me, Ryan, the more actual privacy I have."

"And your privacy is important to you."

"When you grow up the way I did, you learn to value it."

Pressing her face to his chest, Ryan clung to him. Pierce put his hand under her chin and lifted it. Her eyes were already glistening with tears.

"Ryan," he said carefully, "there's no need for you to feel sorry for me."

"No." She shook her head, understanding his reluctance to accept sympathy. It had been the same with Bess. "I know that, but it's difficult not to feel sorry for a small boy."

He smiled, brushing a finger over her lips. "He was very resilient." He set her away from him. "You'd better turn those steaks."

Ryan busied herself with the steaks, knowing he wanted the subject dropped. How could she explain she was hungry for any detail of his life, anything that would bring him closer to her? And perhaps she was wrong, she thought, to touch on the past when she was afraid to touch on the future.

"How do you like them cooked?" she asked as she bent down to the broiler.

"*Mmm,* medium rare." He was more interested in the view she provided as she leaned over. "Link has his own dressing made up for the salad. It's quite good."

"Where did he learn to cook?" she asked as she turned the second steak.

"It was a matter of necessity," Pierce told her. "He likes to eat. Things were lean in the early days when we were on the road. It turned out he was a lot more handy with a can of soup than Bess or me."

Ryan turned and sent him a smile. "You know, they were going to San Francisco today."

"Yes." He quirked a brow. "So?"

"He's just as crazy about her as she is about him."

"I know that, too."

"You might have done something to move things along after all these years," she stated, gesturing with the kitchen fork. "After all, they're your friends."

"Which is exactly why I don't interfere," he said mildly. "What did you do?"

"Well, I didn't interfere," she said with a sniff. "I merely gave him a very gentle shove in the right direction. I mentioned that Bess has a preference for piano players."

"I see."

"He's so shy," she said in exasperation. "He'll be ready for social security before he works up the nerve to—to..."

"To what?" Pierce asked, grinning.

"To anything," Ryan stated. "And stop leering at me."

"Was I?"

"You know very well you were. And anyway—" She gasped and dropped the kitchen fork with a clatter when something brushed past her ankles.

"It's just Circe," Pierce pointed out, then grinned as Ryan sighed. "She smells the meat." He picked up the fork to rinse it off while the cat rubbed against Ryan's legs and purred lovingly. "She'll do her best to convince you she deserves some for herself."

"Your pets have a habit of catching me off guard."

"Sorry." But he smiled, not looking sorry at all.

Ryan put her hands on her hips. "You like to see me rattled, don't you?"

"I like to see you," he answered simply. He laughed and caught her up in his arms. "Though I have to admit, there's something appealing about seeing you wear my clothes while you putter around the kitchen in your bare feet."

"Oh," she said knowingly. "The caveman syndrome."

"Oh, no, Miss Swan." He nuzzled her neck. "I'm your slave."

"Really?" Ryan considered the interesting possibilities of the statement. "Then set the table," she told him. "I'm starving."

They ate by candlelight. Ryan never tasted a mouthful of the meal. She was too full of Pierce. There was wine—something smooth and mellow, but it might have been water, for all it mattered. In the baggy sweatshirt and jeans, she had never felt more like a woman. His eyes told her constantly that she was beautiful, interesting, desirable. It seemed as though they had never been lovers, never been intimate. He was wooing her.

He made her glow with a look, with a soft word or the touch of his hand on hers. It never ceased to please her, even overwhelm her, that he had so much romance in him. He had to know that she would be with him under any circumstances, yet he courted her. Flowers and candlelight and the words of a man captivated. Ryan fell in love again.

Long after both of them had lost any interest in the meal, they lingered. The wine grew warm, the candles low. He was content to watch her in the flickering light, to let her quiet voice flow over him. Whatever needs built inside him could be soothed by merely running his fingers over the back of her hand. He wanted nothing more than to be with her.

Passion would come later, he knew. In the night, in the dark when she lay beside him. But for now it was enough to see her smile.

"Will you wait for me in the parlor?" he murmured and kissed her fingers one at a time. Shivery delight shot up her arm.

"I'll help with the dishes." But her thoughts were far, far away from practical matters.

"No, I'll see to it." Pierce turned her hand over and pressed his lips to her palm. "Wait for me."

Her knees trembled, but she rose when he drew her to her feet. She couldn't take her eyes from his. "You won't be long?"

"No." He slid his hands down her arms. "I won't be long, love." Gently, he kissed her.

Ryan walked to the parlor in a daze. It hadn't been the kiss but the one simple word of endearment that had her heart pounding. It seemed impossible, after what they had been to each other, that a casual word would send her pulses racing. But Pierce was careful with words.

And it was a night for enchantment, she thought as she entered the parlor. A night made for love and romance. She walked to the window to look out at the sky. Even the moon was full, as if it knew it had to be. It was quiet enough that she could just hear the sound of waves against rock.

They were on an island, Ryan imagined. It was a small, windswept island in some dark sea. And the nights were long. There was no phone, no electricity. On impulse, she turned from the window and began to light the candles that were scattered around the room. The fire was laid, and she set a match to the kindling. The dry wood caught with a crackle.

Rising, she looked around the room. The light was just as she wanted it—insubstantial with shadows shifting. It added just a touch of mystery and seemed to reflect her own feelings toward Pierce.

Ryan glanced down at herself and brushed at the sweatshirt. If only she had something lovely to wear, something white and filmy. But perhaps Pierce's imagination would be as active as hers.

Music, she thought suddenly and looked around. Surely he had a stereo, but she wouldn't have any idea where to look for it. Inspired, she went to the piano.

Link's staff paper was waiting. Between the glow from the fire behind her and the candles on the piano,

Ryan could see the notes clearly enough. Sitting down, she began to play. It took only moments for her to be caught up in the melody.

Pierce stood in the doorway and watched her. Although her eyes were fixed on the paper in front of her, they seemed to be dreaming. He'd never seen her quite like this—so caught up in her own thoughts. Unwilling to break her mood, he stood where he was. He could have watched her forever.

In the candlelight her hair was only a mist falling over her shoulders. Her skin was pale. Only her eyes were dark, moved by the music she played. He caught the faint whiff of wood smoke and melting wax. It was a moment he knew he would remember for the rest of his life. Years and years could pass, and he would be able to close his eyes and see her just like this, hear the music drifting, smell the candles burning.

"Ryan." He hadn't meant to speak aloud, indeed had only whispered her name, but her eyes lifted to his.

She smiled, but the flickering light caught the glistening tears. "It's so beautiful."

"Yes." Pierce could hardly trust himself to speak. A word, a wrong move might shatter the mood. What he saw, what he felt might be an illusion after all. "Please, play it again."

Even after she had begun, he came no closer. He wanted the picture to remain exactly as it was. Her lips were just parted. He could taste them as he stood there. He knew how her cheek would feel if he laid his hand on it. She would look up at him and smile with that special warmth in her eyes. But he wouldn't touch her, only absorb all she was in this one special moment out of time.

The flames of the candles burned straight. A log shifted quietly in the grate. And then she was finished.

Her eyes lifted to his. Pierce went to her.

"I've never wanted you more," he said in a low, almost whispering voice. "Or been more afraid to touch you."

"Afraid?" Her fingers stayed lightly on the keys. "Why?"

"If I were to touch you, my hand might pass through you. You might only be a dream after all."

Ryan took his hand and pressed it to her cheek. "It's no dream," she murmured. "Not for either of us."

Her skin was warm and real under his fingers. He was struck by a wave of incredible tenderness. Pierce lifted her other hand, holding it as though it were made of porcelain. "If you had one wish, Ryan, only one, what would it be?"

"That tonight, just tonight, you'd think of nothing and no one but me."

Her eyes were brilliant in the dim, shifting light. Pierce drew her to her feet, then cupped her face in his hand. "You waste your wishes, Ryan, asking for something that already is." He kissed her temples, then her cheeks, leaving her mouth trembling for the taste of his.

"I want to fill your mind," she told him, her voice wavering, "so there's no room for anything else. Tonight I want there to be only me. And tomorrow—"

*"Shh."* He kissed her mouth to silence her, but so lightly she was left with only a promise of what was to come. "There's no one but you, Ryan." Her eyes were closed, and he brushed his lips delicately over the lids. "Come to bed," he murmured. "Let me show you."

Taking her hand, he walked through the room, putting out the candles. He lifted one, letting its quivering light show them the way.

# Chapter Fourteen

They had to be separated again. Ryan knew it was necessary in the course of preparing the special. When she was lonely for him, she had only to remember that last magic night they had spent together. It would be enough to hold her until she could see him again.

Though she saw him off and on during the next weeks, it was only professionally. He came to her for meetings or to oversee certain points of his own business. He kept to himself on these. Ryan still knew nothing about the construction of the props and gags he would use. He would give her a detailed list of the illusions he would perform, their time sequence and only the barest explanation of their mechanics.

Ryan found this frustrating, but she had little else to complain about. The set was forming along the lines she, Bloomfield and Pierce had ultimately agreed on. Elaine Fisher was signed for a guest appearance. Ryan had managed to hold her own through the series of tough, emotional meetings. And so, she recalled with amusement, had Pierce.

He could say more with his long silences and one or two calm words than a dozen frantic, bickering department heads. He sat through their demands and complaints with complete amiability and always came out on top.

He wouldn't agree to use a professional script for the show. It was as simple as that. He said no. And he had stuck to it—because he knew he was right. He had his own music, his own director, his own prop crew. Nothing would sway him from using his own people on key posts. He turned down six costume sketches with a careless shake of the head.

Pierce did things his own way and bent only when it suited him to bend. Yet Ryan saw that the creative staff, as temperamental as they came, offered little complaint about him. He charmed them, she noted. He had a way with people. He would warm you or freeze you—it only took a look.

Bess was to have the final say on her own wardrobe. Pierce simply stated that she knew best what suited her. He refused to rehearse unless the set was closed. Then he entertained the stagehands with sleight of hand and card tricks. He knew how to keep control without rippling the waters.

Ryan, however, found it difficult to function around the restrictions he put on her and her staff. She tried reasoning, arguing, pleading. She got nowhere.

"Pierce." Ryan cornered him on the set during a break in rehearsal. "I have to talk to you."

*"Hmm?"* He watched his crew set up the torches for the next segment. "Exactly eight inches apart," he told them.

"Pierce, this is important."

"Yes, I'm listening."

"You can't bar Ned from the set during rehearsal," she said and tugged on his arm to get his full attention.

"Yes, I can. I did. Didn't he tell you?"

"Yes, he told me." She let out a sigh of exasperation. "Pierce, as production coordinator, he has a perfectly legitimate reason to be here."

"He gets in the way. Make sure there's a foot between the rows, please."

"Pierce!"

"What?" he said pleasantly and turned back to her. "Have I told you that you look lovely today, Miss Swan?" He ran the lapel of her jacket between his thumb and forefinger. "That's a very nice suit."

"Listen, Pierce, you've got to give my people a little more room." She tried to ignore the smile in his eyes and continued. "Your crew is very efficient, but on a production of this size we need more hands. Your people know your work, but they don't know television."

"I can't have your people poking into my props, Ryan. Or wandering around when I'm setting up."

"Good grief, do you want them to sign a blood oath not to reveal your secrets?" she demanded, waving her clipboard. "We could set it up for the next full moon."

"A good idea, but I don't know how many of your people would go along with it. Not your production coordinator, at any rate," he added with a grin. "I don't think he'd care for the sight of his own blood."

Ryan lifted a brow. "Are you jealous?"

He laughed with such great enjoyment she wanted to hit him. "Don't be absurd. He's hardly a threat."

"That's not the point," she muttered, miffed. "He's very good at his job, but he can hardly do it if you won't be reasonable."

"Ryan," he said, looking convincingly surprised, "I'm always reasonable. What would you like me to do?"

"I'd like you to let Ned do what he has to do. And I'd like you to let my people in the studio."

"Certainly," he agreed. "But not when I'm rehearsing."

"Pierce," she said dangerously. "You're tying my hands. You have to make certain concessions for television."

"I'm aware of that, Ryan, and I will." He kissed her brow. "When I'm ready. No," he continued before she could speak again, "you have to let me work with my own crew until I'm sure it's smooth."

"And how long is that going to take?" She knew he was winning her over as he had everyone from Coogar down.

"A few more days." He took her free hand. "Your key people are here, in any case."

"All right," she said with a sigh. "But by the end of the week the lighting crew will have to be in on rehearsals. That's essential."

"Agreed." He gave her hand a solemn shake. "Anything else?"

"Yes." Ryan straightened her shoulders and shot him a level look. "The time for the first segment runs over by ten seconds. You're going to have to alter it to fit the scheduled run of the commercials."

"No, you'll have to alter the scheduled run of commercials." He gave her a light kiss before he walked away.

Before she could shout at him, Ryan found there was a rosebud pinned to her lapel. Pleasure mixed with fury until it was too late to act.

"He's something, isn't he?"

Ryan turned her head to see Elaine Fisher. "Something," she agreed. "I hope you're satisfied with everything, Miss Fisher," she continued, then smiled at the petite, kittenlike blonde. "Your dressing room's agreeable?"

"It's fine." Elaine flashed her winning, toothy smile. "There's a bulb burned out on my mirror, though."

"I'll see to it."

Elaine watched Pierce and gave her quick, bubbling laugh. "I've got to tell you, I wouldn't mind finding him in my dressing room."

"I don't think I can arrange that for you, Miss Fisher," Ryan returned primly.

"Oh, honey, I could arrange it for myself if it weren't for the way he looks at you." She sent Ryan a friendly wink. "Of course, if you're not interested, I could try to console him."

The actress's charm wasn't easy to resist. "That won't be necessary," Ryan told her with a smile. "It's a producer's job to keep the talent happy, you know."

"Why don't you see if you could come up with a clone for me?" Leaving Ryan, she walked to Pierce. "Ready for me?"

Watching them work together, Ryan saw that her instincts had been on the mark. They were perfectly suited. Elaine's frothy blond beauty and ingenue charm masked a sharp talent and flair for comedy. It was the exact balance Ryan had hoped for.

Ryan waited, holding her breath as the torches were lit. It was the first time she had seen the illusion all the way through. The flames burned high for a moment, sending out an almost blinding light before Pierce spread his hands and calmed them. Then he turned to Elaine.

"Don't burn the dress," she cracked. "It's rented."

Ryan scribbled down a note to keep in the ad lib even as he began to levitate Elaine. In moments she was floating just above the flames.

"It's going well."

Glancing up, Ryan smiled at Bess. "Yes, for all the problems he causes, Pierce makes it impossible for it to go otherwise. He's relentless."

"Tell me about it." They watched him in silence a moment, then Bess squeezed Ryan's arm. "I can't stand it," she said in undertones to keep from disturbing the rehearsal. "I have to tell you."

"Tell me what?"

"I wanted to tell Pierce first, but..." She grinned from ear to ear. "Link and I—"

"Oh, congratulations!" Ryan interrupted and hugged her.

Bess laughed. "You didn't let me finish."

"You were going to tell me you're getting married."

"Well, yeah, but—"

"Congratulations," Ryan said again. "When did it happen?"

"Just now, practically." Looking a little dazed, Bess scratched her head. "I was in my dressing room getting ready when he knocked on the door. He wouldn't come in, he just stood there in the doorway sort of shuffling his feet, you know? Then all of a sudden he asked me if I wanted to get married." Bess shook her head and laughed again. "I was so surprised, I asked him to whom."

"Oh, Bess, you didn't!"

"Yeah, I did. Well, you just don't expect that sort of question after twenty years."

"Poor Link," Ryan murmured with a smile. "What did he say?"

"He just stood there for a minute, staring at me and turning colors, then he said, 'Well, to me, I guess.'" She gave a low chuckle. "It was real romantic."

"I think it was lovely," Ryan told her. "I'm so happy for you."

"Thanks." After a breathy sigh, she looked over at Pierce again. "Don't say anything to Pierce, okay? I think I'll let Link tell him."

"I won't say anything," she promised. "Will you be married soon?"

Bess sent her a lopsided grin. "Sweetie, you better believe it. As far as I can see, we've already been engaged for twenty years, and that's long enough." She pleated the hem of her sweatshirt between her fingers. "I guess we'll just wait until after the special airs, then make the jump."

"Will you stay with Pierce?"

"Sure." She looked at Ryan quizzically. "We're a team. 'Course, Link and I will live at my place, but we wouldn't break up the act."

"Bess," Ryan began slowly. "There's something I've been wanting to ask you. It's about the final illusion." She sent Pierce a worried frown as he continued to work with Elaine. "He's so secretive about it. All he'll say so far is that it's an escape and he'll need four minutes and ten seconds from intro to finish. What do you know about it?"

Bess shrugged restlessly. "He's keeping that one close because he hasn't worked out all the bugs."

"What sort of bugs?" Ryan persisted.

"I don't know, really, except..." She hesitated, torn between her own doubts and her loyalty. "Except Link doesn't like it."

"Why?" Ryan put a hand on Bess's arm. "Is it dangerous? Really dangerous?"

"Look, Ryan, all the escapes can be dangerous, unless you're talking a straightjacket and handcuffs. But he's the best." She watched Pierce lower Elaine to the floor. "He's going to need me in a minute."

"Bess." She kept her hand firm on the redhead's arm. "Tell me what you know."

"Ryan." Bess sighed as she looked down at her. "I know how you feel about him, but I can't. Pierce's work is Pierce's work."

"I'm not asking you to break the magician's code of ethics," Ryan said impatiently. "He'll have to tell me what the illusion is, anyway."

"Then he'll tell you." Bess patted her hand but moved away.

The rehearsals ran over, as Pierce's rehearsals had a habit of doing. After attending a late afternoon production meeting, Ryan decided to wait for him in his dressing room. The problem of the final illusion had nagged at her throughout the day. She hadn't liked the worried look in Bess's eyes.

Pierce's dressing room was spacious and plush. The carpeting was thick, the sofa plump and wide enough to double as a bed. There was a large-screen television, a complex stereo system and a fully stocked bar that she knew Pierce never used. On the wall were a pair of very good lithographs. It was the sort of dressing room Swan reserved for their special performers. Ryan doubted that Pierce spent more than thirty minutes a day within its walls when he was in L.A.

Ryan poked in the refrigerator, found a quart of orange juice and fixed herself a cold drink before sinking down on the sofa. Idly, she picked up a book from the table. It was one of Pierce's, she noted, another work on Houdini. With absent interest she thumbed through the pages.

When Pierce entered, he found her curled up on the sofa, halfway through the volume.

"Research?"

Ryan's head shot up. "Could he really do all these things?" she demanded. "I mean this business about swallowing needles and a ball of thread, then pulling them out threaded. He didn't really do that, did he?"

"Yes." He stripped out of his shirt.

Ryan gave him a narrowed look. "Can you?"

He only smiled. "I don't make a habit of copying illusions. How was your day?"

"Fine. It says in here that some people thought he had a pocket in his skin."

This time he laughed. "Don't you think you'd have found mine by now if I had one?"

Ryan set the book aside and rose. "I want to talk to you."

"All right." Pierce pulled her into his arms and began to roam her face with kisses. "In a few minutes. It's been a long three days without you."

"You were the one who went away," she reminded him, then halted his wandering mouth with her own.

"I had a few details to smooth out. I can't work seriously here."

"That's what your dungeon's for," she murmured and found his mouth again.

"Exactly. We'll go to dinner tonight. Some place with candles and dark corners."

"My apartment has candles and dark corners," she said against his lips. "We can be alone there."

"You'll try to seduce me again."

Ryan laughed and forgot what she had wanted to talk to him about. "I *will* seduce you again."

"You've gotten cocky, Miss Swan." He drew her away. "I'm not always so easy."

"I like challenges."

He rubbed his nose against hers. "Did you like your flower?"

"Yes, thank you." She circled his neck with her arms. "It kept me from harassing you."

"I know. You find me difficult to work with, don't you?"

"Extremely. And if you let anyone else produce your next special, I'll sabotage every one of your illusions."

"Well, then, I'll have to keep you and protect myself."

He touched his lips to hers gently, and the wave of love hit her with such force, such suddenness, Ryan clutched at him.

"Pierce." She wanted to speak quickly before the old fear prevented her. "Pierce, read my mind." With her eyes tightly shut, she buried her face against his shoulder. "Can you read my mind?"

Puzzled by the urgency in her tone, he drew her away to study her. She opened her eyes wide, and in them he saw that she was a little frightened, a little dazed. And he saw something else that had his heart taking an erratic beat.

"Ryan?" Pierce lifted a hand to her cheek, afraid he was seeing something only he needed to see. Afraid, too, that it was real.

"I'm terrified," she whispered. "The words won't come. Can you see them?" Her voice was jerky. She bit her lip to steady it. "If you can't, I'll understand. It doesn't have to change anything."

Yes, he saw them, but she was wrong. Once they were said, they changed everything. He hadn't wanted it to happen, yet he had known, somehow, they would come to this. He had known the moment he had seen her walk down the steps to his workroom. She was the woman who would change everything. Whatever power he had would become partially hers once he said three words. It was the only real incantation in a world of illusion.

"Ryan." He hesitated a moment but knew there was no stopping what already was. "I love you."

Her breath came out in a rush of relief. "Oh, Pierce, I was so afraid you wouldn't want to see." They drew together and clung. "I love you so much. So very much." Her sigh was shaky. "It's good, isn't it?"

"Yes." He felt her heartbeat match his own. "Yes, it's good."

"I didn't know I could be so happy. I wanted to tell you before," she murmured against his throat. "But I was so afraid. It seems silly now."

"We were both afraid." He drew her closer, but it still wasn't enough. "We've wasted time."

"But you love me," she whispered, only wanting to hear the words again.

"Yes, Ryan, I love you."

"Let's go home, Pierce." She ran her lips along his jaw. "Let's go home. I want you."

"Uh-uh. Now."

Ryan threw her head back and laughed. "Now? Here?"

"Here and now," he agreed, enjoying the flash of devilment in her eyes.

"Somebody might come in," she said and drew away from him.

Saying nothing, Pierce turned to the door and flicked the lock. "I don't think so."

"Oh." Ryan bit her lip, trying not to smile. "It looks like I'm going to be ravished."

"You could call for help," he suggested as he pushed the jacket from her shoulders.

"Help," she said quietly while he unbuttoned her blouse. "I don't think anyone heard me."

"Then it looks like you're going to be ravished."

"Oh, good," Ryan whispered. Her blouse slid to the floor.

They touched each other and laughed with the sheer joy of being in love. They kissed and clung as though there were no tomorrow. They murmured soft words and sighed with pleasure. Even when the lovemaking intensified and passion began to rule, there was an underlying joy that remained innocent.

*He loves me,* Ryan thought and ran her hands up his strong back. *He belongs to me.* She answered his kiss with fervor.

*She loves me,* Pierce thought and felt her skin heat under his fingers. *She belongs to me.* He sought her mouth and savored it.

They gave to each other, took from each other until they were more one than two. There was rising passion, an infinite tenderness and a new freedom. When the loving was over, they could still laugh, dizzy with the knowledge that for them it was only the beginning.

"You know," Ryan murmured, "I thought it was the producer who lured the talent to the couch."

"Didn't you?" Pierce let her hair run through his fingers.

With a chuckle Ryan kissed him between the eyes. "You were supposed to think it was all your idea." Sitting up, she reached for her blouse.

Pierce sat up behind her and ran a fingertip up her spine. "Going somewhere?"

"Look, Atkins, you'll get your screen test." She squealed when he bit her shoulder. "Don't try to change my mind," she said before she slipped out of reach. "I'm finished with you."

"Oh?" Pierce leaned back on his elbow to watch her dress.

"Until we get home." Ryan wriggled into her teddy, then began to hook her stockings. She eyed his nakedness. "You'd better get dressed before I change my mind. We'll end up locked in the building for the night."

"I could get us out when we wanted to go."

"There are alarms."

He laughed. "Ryan, really."

She shot him a look. "I suppose it is a good thing you decided not to be a criminal."

"It's simpler to charge for picking locks. People will always find a fascination in paying to see if it can be done." He grinned as he sat up. "They don't appreciate it if you do it for free."

Curious, she tilted her head. "Have you ever come across a lock you can't beat?"

"Given enough time," Pierce said as he reached for his clothes, "any lock can be opened."

"Without tools?"

He lifted a brow. "There are tools, and there are tools."

Ryan frowned at him. "I'm going to have to check for that pocket in your skin again."

"Anytime," he agreed obligingly.

"You could be nice and teach me just one thing, like how to get out of those handcuffs."

"Uh-uh." He shook his head as he slipped into his jeans. "They might come in handy again."

Ryan shrugged as if she didn't care anyway and began to button her blouse. "Oh, I forgot. I wanted to talk to you about the finale."

Pierce pulled a fresh shirt out of the closet. "What about it?"

"That's precisely what I want to know," Ryan told him. "What exactly do you have planned?"

"It's an escape, I told you." He drew on the shirt.

"I need more than that, Pierce. The show goes on in ten days."

"I'm working it out."

Recognizing the tone, Ryan stepped to him. "No, this isn't a solo production. I'm the producer, Pierce; you wanted it that way. Now, I can go along with some of your oddities about the staff." She ignored his indignant expression. "But I have to know exactly what's going to be aired. You can't keep me in the dark with less than two weeks to go until taping."

"I'm going to break out of a safe," he said simply and handed Ryan her shoe.

"Break out of a safe." She took it, watching him. "There's more to it than that, Pierce. I'm not a fool."

"I'll have my hands and feet manacled first."

Ryan stooped to retrieve her other shoe. His continued reluctance to elaborate brought on a very real fear. Wanting her voice to be steady, she waited a moment. "What else, Pierce?"

He said nothing until he had buttoned his shirt. "It's a play on a box within a box within a box. An old gimmick."

The fear grew. "Three safes? One within the other?"

"That's right. Each one's larger than the last."

"Are the safes airtight?"

"Yes."

Ryan's skin grew cold. "I don't like it."

He gave her a calm measuring look. "You don't have to like it, Ryan, but you don't have to worry, either."

She swallowed, knowing it was important to keep her head. "There's more, too, isn't there? I know there is, tell me."

"The last safe has a time lock," he said flatly. "I've done it before."

"A time lock?" Ice ran down her back. "No, you can't. It's just foolish."

"Hardly foolish," Pierce returned. "It's taken me months to work out the mechanics and timing."

"Timing?"

"I have three minutes of air."

*Three minutes!* she thought and struggled not to lose control. "And how long does the escape take?"

"At the moment, just over three minutes."

"Just over," Ryan repeated numbly. "Just over. What if something goes wrong?"

"I don't intend for anything to go wrong. I've been over and over it, Ryan."

She spun away, then whirled back to him. "I'm not going to allow this. It's out of the question. Use the panther business for the finale, but not this."

"I'm using the escape, Ryan." His voice was very calm and very final.

"No!" Panicked, she grabbed his arms. "I'm cutting it. It's out, Pierce. You can use one of your other illusions or come up with a new one, but this is out."

"You can't cut it." His tone never altered as he looked down at her. "I have final say; read the contract."

She paled and stepped back from him. "Damn you, I don't care about the contract. I know what it says. I wrote it!"

"Then you know you can't cut the escape," he said quietly.

"I won't let you do this." Tears had sprung to her eyes, but she blinked them away. "You can't do it."

"I'm sorry, Ryan."

"I'll find a way to scrub the show." Her breath was heaving with anger and fear and hopelessness. "I can find a way to break the contract."

"Maybe." He laid his hands on her shoulders. "I'll still do the escape, Ryan, next month in New York."

"Pierce, God!" Desperately, she clung to his arms. "You could die in there. It's not worth it. Why do you have to try something like this?"

"Because I can do it. Ryan, understand that this is my work."

"I understand that I love you. Doesn't that matter?"

"You know that it does," he said roughly. "You know how much."

"No, I don't know how much." Frantically, she pushed away from him. "I only know that you're going to do this no matter how much I beg you not to. You'll expect me to stand by and watch you risk your life for some applause and a write-up."

"It has nothing to do with applause or write-ups." The first hint of anger shot into his eyes. "You should know me better than that."

"No, no, I don't know you," she said desperately. "How can I understand why you insist on doing something like this? It's not necessary to the show, to your career!"

He struggled to hold his temper in check and answered calmly. "It's necessary to me."

"Why?" she demanded furiously. "Why is it necessary to risk your life?"

"That's your viewpoint, Ryan, not mine. This is part of my work and part of what I am." He paused but didn't go to her. "You'll have to accept that if you accept me."

"That's not fair."

"Maybe not," he agreed. "I'm sorry."

Ryan swallowed, fighting back tears. "Where does that leave us?"

He kept his eyes on hers. "That's up to you."

"I won't watch." She backed to the door. "I won't! I won't spend my life waiting for the time you go too far. I can't." She fumbled for the lock with trembling fingers. "Damn your magic," she sobbed as she darted through the door.

# Chapter Fifteen

After leaving Pierce, Ryan went straight to her father's office. For the first time in her life she entered without knocking. Annoyed at the interruption, Swan bit off what he was saying into the phone and scowled up at her. For a moment he stared at her. He'd never seen Ryan like this: pale, trembling, her eyes wide and brilliant with suppressed tears.

"I'll get back to you," he muttered and hung up. She still stood by the door, and Swan found himself in the unusual position of not knowing what to say. "What is it?" he demanded, then cleared his throat.

Ryan supported herself against the door until she was sure her legs were steady enough to walk. Struggling for composure, she crossed to her father's desk. "I need—I want you to cancel the Atkins special."

"What!" He sprang to his feet and glared at her. "What the hell is this? If you've decided to fall apart under the pressure, I'll get a replacement. Ross can take over. Damn it!" He slammed his hand on the desk. "I should have known better than to put you in charge in the first place." He was already reaching for the phone.

"Please." Ryan's quiet voice stopped him. "I'm asking you to pay off the contract and scrub the show."

Swan started to swear at her again, took another careful study of her face, then walked to the bar. Saying nothing, he poured a healthy dose of French brandy into a snifter. Blast the girl for making him feel like a clumsy ox. "Here," he said gruffly as he pushed the snifter into her hands. "Sit down and drink this." Not certain what to do with a daughter who looked shattered and helpless, he awkwardly patted her shoulder before he went back behind his desk.

"Now." Settled again, he felt more in control of the situation. "Tell me what this is all about. Trouble at rehearsals?" He gave her what he hoped was an understanding smile. "Now, you've been around the business long enough to know that's part of the game."

Ryan took a deep breath, then swallowed the brandy. She let it burn through the layers of fear and misery. Her next breath was steadier. She looked at her father again. "Pierce is planning an escape for the finale."

"I know that," he said impatiently. "I've seen the script."

"It's too dangerous."

"Dangerous?" Swan folded his hands on the desk. This he could handle, he decided. "Ryan, the man's a pro. He knows what he's doing." Swan tilted his wrist slightly so he could see his watch. He could give her about five minutes.

"This is different," she insisted. To keep from screaming, she gripped the bowl of the snifter tightly. Swan would never listen to hysterics. "Even his own people don't like it."

"All right, what's he planning?"

Unable to form the words, Ryan took another swallow of brandy. "Three safes," she began. "One within the other. The last one..." she paused for a moment to keep her voice even. "The last one has a time lock. He'll only have three minutes of air once he's closed inside the first safe. He's just—he's just told me that the routine takes more time than that.''

''Three safes,'' Swan mused, pursing his lips. ''A real show-stopper.''

Ryan slammed down her glass. ''Especially if he suffocates. Think what that will do for the ratings! They can give him his Emmy posthumously.''

Swan lowered his brows dangerously. ''Calm down, Ryan.''

''I will not calm down.'' She sprang up from her chair. ''He can't be allowed to do this. We have to cancel the contract.''

''Can't do it.'' Swan lifted his shoulders to brush off the notion.

''Won't do it,'' Ryan corrected furiously.

''Won't do it,'' Swan agreed, matching her tone. ''There's too much at stake.''

''*Everything's* at stake!'' Ryan shouted at him. ''I'm in love with him.''

He had started to stand and shout back at her, but her words took him by surprise. Swan stared at her. There were tears of desperation in her eyes now. Again he was at a loss. ''Ryan.'' He sighed and reached for a cigar. ''Sit down.''

''No!'' She snatched the cigar from his fingers and flung it across the room. ''I will not sit down, I will not calm down. I'm asking for your help. Why won't you look at me?'' she demanded in angry despair. ''Really look at me!''

''I am looking at you!'' he bellowed in defense. ''And I can tell you I'm not pleased. Now you sit down and listen to me.''

''No, I'm through listening to you, trying to please you. I've done everything you've ever wanted me to do, but it's never been enough. I can't be your son, I can't change that." She covered her face with her hands and broke down completely. "I'm only your daughter, and I need you to help me."

The words left him speechless. The tears unmanned him. He couldn't remember if he had ever seen her cry before; certainly she'd never done it this passionately. Getting awkwardly to his feet, he fumbled for his handkerchief. "Here, here now." He pushed the handkerchief into her hands and wondered what to do next. "I've always..." He cleared his throat and looked helplessly around the room. "I've always been proud of you, Ryan." When she responded by weeping more desperately, he stuck his hands in his pockets and lapsed into silence.

"It doesn't matter." Her voice was muffled behind the handkerchief. She felt a wave of shame for the words and the tears. "It doesn't matter anymore."

"I'd help you if I could," he muttered at length. "I can't stop him. Even if I could scrub the show and deal with the suits the network and Atkins would bring against Swan Productions, he'd do the damn thing anyway."

Faced with the bald truth, Ryan turned away from him. "There must be something..."

Swan shifted uncomfortably. "Is he in love with you?"

Ryan let out an unsteady breath and dashed the tears away. "It doesn't matter how he feels about me. I can't stop him."

"I'll talk to him."

Wearily, she shook her head. "No, it wouldn't do any good. I'm sorry." She turned back to her father. "I shouldn't have come here like this. I wasn't thinking straight." Looking down, she crumpled the handkerchief into a ball. "I'm sorry I made a scene."

"Ryan, I'm your father."

She looked up at him then, but her eyes were expressionless. "Yes."

He cleared his throat and found he didn't know what to do with his hands. "I don't want you to apologize for coming to see me." She only continued to look at him with eyes devoid of emotion. Tentatively, he reached out to touch her arm. "I'll do what I can to persuade Atkins to drop the routine, if that's what you want."

Ryan let out a long sigh before she sat down. "Thank you, but you were right. He'll do it another time, anyway. He told me so himself. I'm just not able to deal with it."

"Do you want Ross to take over?"

She pressed her fingers to her eyes. "No," she said with a shake of her head. "No, I'll finish what I started. Hiding won't change anything, either."

"Good girl," he said with a pleased nod. "Now, ah..." He hesitated while he sought the correct words. "About you and the magician." He coughed and fiddled with his tie. "Are you planning—that is, should I talk to him about his intentions?"

Ryan hadn't thought she could smile. "No, that won't be necessary." She saw relief in Swan's eyes and rose. "I'd appreciate some time off after the taping."

"Of course, you've earned it."

"I won't keep you any longer." She started to turn away, but he put a hand on her shoulder. Ryan glanced at him in surprise.

"Ryan..." He couldn't get a clear hold on what he wanted to say to her. Instead, he squeezed her shoulder. "Come on, I'll take you to dinner."

Ryan stared at him. When was the last time, she wondered, she had gone to dinner with her father? An awards banquet? A business party? "Dinner?" she said blankly.

"Yes." Swan's voice sharpened as his thoughts followed the same path Ryan's had. "A man can take his daughter to dinner, can't he?" He slipped his arm around her waist and led her to the door. How small she was! he realized with a jolt. "Go wash your face," he muttered. "I'll wait for you."

At ten o'clock the next morning Swan finished reading the Atkins contract a second time. A tricky business, he thought. It wouldn't be easy to break. But he had no intention of breaking it. That would not only be poor business sense but a useless gesture. He'd just have to deal with Atkins himself. When his buzzer sounded, he turned the contract facedown.

"Mr. Atkins is here, Mr. Swan."

"Send him in."

Swan rose as Pierce entered, and as he had done the first time, he walked across the room with his hand extended. "Pierce," he said jovially. "Thanks for coming up."

"Mr. Swan."

"Bennett, please," he said as he drew Pierce to a chair.

"Bennett," Pierce agreed, taking a seat.

Swan sat in the chair opposite him and leaned back. "Well, now, are you satisfied with how everything's going?"

Pierce lifted a brow. "Yes."

Swan took out a cigar. The man's too cool, he thought grudgingly. He doesn't give anything away. Swan decided to approach the subject from the side door. "Coogar tells me the rehearsals are smooth as silk. Worries him." Swan grinned. "He's a superstitious bastard, likes plenty of trouble before a taping. He tells me you could almost run the show yourself."

"He's a fine director," Pierce said easily, watching Swan light his cigar.

"The best," Swan agreed heartily. "We are a bit concerned about your plans for the finale."

"Oh?"

"This is television, you know," Swan reminded him with an expansive smile. "Four-ten is a bit long for one routine."

"It's necessary." Pierce let his hands rest on the arms of the chair. "I'm sure Ryan's told you."

Swan's eyes met the direct stare. "Yes, Ryan's told me. She came up here last night. She was frantic."

Pierce's fingers tensed slightly, but he kept his eyes level. "I know. I'm sorry."

"Look, Pierce, we're reasonable men." Swan leaned toward him, poking with his cigar. "This routine of yours sounds like a beauty. The time lock business is a real inspiration, but with a little modification—"

"I don't modify my illusions."

The cool dismissal had Swan blustering. "No contract's carved in stone," he said dangerously.

"You can try to break it," Pierce agreed. "It'll be a great deal more trouble for you than for me. And in the end it won't change anything."

"Damn it, man, the girl's beside herself!" Banging his thigh with his fist, Swan flopped back in the chair. "She says she's in love with you."

"She is in love with me," Pierce returned quietly and ignored the twist in his stomach.

"What the hell do you mean to do about it?"

"Are you asking me as her father or as Swan Productions?"

Swan drew his brows together and muttered for a moment. "As her father," he decided.

"I'm in love with Ryan." Pierce met Swan's stare calmly. "If she's willing to have me, I'll spend my life with her."

"And if she's not?" Swan retorted.

Pierce's eyes darkened, something flickered, but he said nothing. That was something he'd yet to deal with. In the brief passage of seconds Swan saw what he wanted to know. He pressed his advantage.

"A woman in love isn't always reasonable," he said with an avuncular smile. "A man has to make certain adjustments."

"There's very little I wouldn't do for Ryan," Pierce returned. "But it isn't possible for me to change what I am."

"We're talking about a routine," Swan tossed back, losing patience.

"No, we're talking about my way of life. I could drop this escape," he continued while Swan frowned at him, "but there'd be another one and still another. If Ryan can't accept this one now, how can she accept one later?"

"You'll lose her," Swan warned.

Pierce rose at that, unable to sit any longer. "Perhaps I've never had her." He could deal with the pain, he told himself. He knew how to deal with pain. His voice was even when he continued. "Ryan has to make her own choices. I have to accept them."

Swan rose to his feet and glared. "Damn if you sound like a man in love to me."

Pierce gave him a long, cold stare that had Swan swallowing. "In a lifetime of illusions," he said roughly, "she's the only thing that's real." Turning, he strode from the room.

# Chapter Sixteen

They would tape at six o'clock west coast time. By 4:00 P.M. Ryan had dealt with everything from an irate property manager to a frazzled hair stylist. There was nothing like a live broadcast to throw even the most seasoned veterans into a state of madness. As it was put to her by a fatalistic stagehand, "Whatever could go wrong, would." It wasn't what Ryan wanted to hear.

But the problems, the demands, the touch of insanity kept her from crawling into a convenient corner to weep. She was needed and had no choice but to be dependable. If her career was all she was going to have left, Ryan knew she had to give it her best shot.

She had avoided Pierce for ten days by keeping an emotional distance. They had no choice but to come together time and again, but only as producer and star. He made no attempt to close the gap between them.

Ryan hurt. At times it still amazed her how much. Still, she welcomed it. The hurt helped smother the fear. The three safes had been delivered. When she had forced herself to examine them, she had seen that the smallest was no more than three feet high and two feet across. The thought of Pierce folding himself into the small black box had her stomach rolling.

She had stood studying the largest safe with its thick door and complex time lock when she had sensed him behind her. When she had turned, they had looked at each other in silence. Ryan had felt the need, the love, the hopelessness before she had walked away from him. Neither by word nor gesture had he asked her to stay.

From then on Ryan had kept away from the safes, concentrating instead on the checking and rechecking of all the minute details of production.

Wardrobe had to be supervised. A broken spotlight needed repair at the eleventh hour. A sick technician had to be replaced. And timing, the most crucial element of all, had to be worked out to the last second.

There seemed to be no end to the last-minute problems, and she could only be grateful when each new one cropped up. There was no time for thinking, right up to the moment when the studio audience began to file in.

With her stomach in knots, her face composed, Ryan waited in the control booth as the floor director gave the final countdown.

It began.

Pierce was onstage, cool and competent. The set was perfect: clean, uncluttered and faintly mysterious with the understated lighting. In unrelieved black, he was a twentieth-century sorcerer with no need for magic wands or pointed hats.

Water flowed between his palms, fire shot from his fingertips. Ryan watched as he balanced Bess on the point of a saber, making her spin like a top, then drawing the sword out with a flourish until she spun on nothing at all.

Elaine floated on the torch flames while the audience held their breath. Pierce enclosed her in a clear glass bubble, covered it with red silk and sent it floating ten feet above the stage. It swayed gently to Link's music. When Pierce brought it down and whipped off the silk, Elaine was a white swan.

He varied his illusions—dashing, spectacular and simply beautiful. He controlled the elements, defied nature and baffled all.

"Going like a dream," Ryan heard someone say excitedly. "See if we don't cop a couple of Emmys for this one. Thirty seconds, camera two. God, is this guy good!"

Ryan left the control booth and went down to the wings. She told herself she was cold because the air-conditioning in the booth was turned up so high. It would be warmer near the stage. The lights there shone hotly, but her skin stayed chilled. She watched while he did a variation on the transportation illusion he had used in Vegas.

He never glanced in her direction, but Ryan sensed he knew she was there. He had to know, because her thoughts were so completely centered on him.

"It's going good, isn't it?"

Looking up, Ryan saw Link beside her. "Yes, perfect so far."

"I liked the swan. It's pretty."

"Yes."

"Maybe you should go into Bess's dressing room and sit down," he suggested, wishing she didn't look so pale and cold. "You could watch on the TV in there."

"No. No, I'll stay."

Pierce had a tiger onstage, a lean, pacing cat in a gilt cage. He covered it with the same silk he had used on the bubble. When he removed it, Elaine was caged and the tiger had vanished. Knowing it was the last illusion before the final escape, Ryan took a deep breath.

"Link." She reached for his hand, needing something to hold onto.

"He'll be all right, Ryan." He gave her fingers a squeeze. "Pierce is the best."

The smallest safe was brought out, its door open wide as it was turned around and around to show its solidity. Ryan tasted the iron tang of fear. She didn't hear Pierce's explanation to the audience as he was manacled hand and foot by a captain of the Los Angeles Police Department. Her eyes were glued to his face. She knew the deepest part of his mind was already locked inside the vault. Already, he was working his way out. That's what she held onto as firmly as Link's hand.

He barely fit inside the first safe. His shoulders brushed the sides.

He won't be able to move in there, she thought on a stab of panic. As the door was shut, she took a step toward the stage. Link held her by the shoulders.

"You can't, Ryan."

"But, God, he can't move. He can't breathe!" She watched with mounting horror as the second safe was brought out.

"He's already out of the cuffs," Link said soothingly, though he didn't like watching the safe that held Pierce lifted and locked inside the second one. "He'll be opening the first door now," he said to comfort himself as much as Ryan. "He works fast. You know, you've seen him."

"Oh, no." The third safe had the fear rocketing almost beyond her control. She felt a bright dizziness and would have swayed if Link's hands hadn't held her upright. The largest safe swallowed the two others and the man inside. It was shut, bolted. The time lock was set for midnight. There was no way in from the outside now.

"How long?" she whispered. Her eyes were glued to the safe, on the shiny, complicated timer. "How long since he's been in?"

"Two and a half minutes." Link felt a bead of sweat run down his back. "He's got plenty of time."

He knew the safes fit together so snugly that the doors could only be pushed open far enough for a child to crawl through. He never understood how Pierce could twist and fold his body the way he did. But he'd seen him do it. Unlike Ryan, Link had watched Pierce rehearse the escape countless times. The sweat continued to roll down his back.

The air was thin, Ryan could barely draw it into her lungs. That was how it was inside the safe, she thought numbly. No air, no light. "Time, Link!" She was shaking like a leaf now. The big man stopped praying to answer.

"Two-fifty. It's almost over. He's working on the last one now."

Gripping her hands together, Ryan began to count off the seconds in her head. The roaring in her ears had her biting down hard on her lip. She had never fainted in her life, but she knew she was perilously close to doing so now. When her vision blurred, she squeezed her eyes tight to clear it. But she couldn't breathe. Pierce had no air now and neither did she. On a bubble of hysteria, she thought she would suffocate standing there as surely as Pierce would inside the trio of safes.

Then she saw the door opening, heard the unified gasp of relief from the audience before the burst of applause. He stood on the stage, damp with sweat and drawing in air.

Ryan swooned back against Link as darkness blocked out the spotlights. She lost consciousness for no more than seconds, coming back when she heard Link calling her.

"Ryan, Ryan, it's all right. He's out. He's okay."

Bracing herself against Link, she shook her head to clear it. "Yes, he's out." For one last second she watched him, then turning, she walked away.

The moment the cameras shut off, Pierce walked offstage. "Where's Ryan?" he demanded of Link.

"She left." He watched a trickle of sweat run down Pierce's face. "She was pretty upset." He offered Pierce the towel he'd been holding for him. "I think maybe she fainted for a minute."

Pierce didn't brush away the sweat, he didn't grin as he always did when an escape was completed. "Where did she go?"

"I don't know. She just left."

Without a word, Pierce went to look for her.

Ryan lay baking in the strong sun. There was an itch in the center of her back, but she didn't move to scratch it. She lay still and let the heat soak into her skin.

She had spent a week on board her father's yacht off the coast of St. Croix. Swan had let her go alone, as she requested, asking no questions when she had arrived at his house and asked for the favor. He'd made the arrangements for her and had taken her to the airport himself. Ryan was to think later that it was the first time he hadn't put her in a limo with a driver and sent her off to catch a plane by herself.

For days now she had lain in the sun, swam and kept her mind a blank. She hadn't even gone back to her apartment after the taping. She had arrived in St. Croix with the clothes on her back. Whatever she needed she bought on the island. She spoke to no one but the crew and sent no messages back to the States. For a week she simply slipped off the face of the earth.

Ryan rolled over on her back and dropped the sunglasses over her eyes. She knew that if she didn't force herself to think, the answer she needed would come to her in time. When it came, it would be right, and she would act on it. Until then, she waited.

In his workroom, Pierce shuffled and cut the Tarot cards. He needed to relax. The tension was eating at him.

After the taping he had searched the entire building for Ryan. When she was nowhere to be found, he had broken one of his own cardinal rules and had picked the lock on her apartment. He had waited for her through the next morning. She had never come home. It had driven him wild, furious. He'd let the rage take him, blocking out the pain. Anger, the undisciplined anger he never allowed himself, came in full force. Link had borne the brunt of his temper in silence.

It had taken Pierce days to regain his control. Ryan was gone, and he had to accept it. His own set of rules left him no choice. Even if he'd known where to find her, he couldn't bring her back.

In the week that had passed he had done no work. He had no power. Whenever he tried to focus his concentration, he saw only Ryan—felt her, tasted her. It was all he could conjure. He had to work his way back.

Pierce knew if he didn't find his rhythm again soon he would be finished.

He was alone now, with Link and Bess honeymooning in the mountains. When he had regained some of his control, he had insisted they keep to their plans. He had sent them on their way, struggling to give them happiness while his own life loomed empty ahead of him.

It was time to go back to the only thing he had left. And even that brought a small trickle of fear. He was no longer sure he had any magic.

Setting the cards aside, Pierce rose to set up one of his more complicated illusions. He wouldn't test himself on anything simplistic. Even as he began to train his concentration, flex his hands, he looked up and saw her.

Pierce stared hard at the image. She had never come this clearly to him before. He could even hear her footsteps as she crossed the room to the stage. Her scent reached him first and had his blood humming. He wondered, almost dispassionately, if he were going mad.

"Hello, Pierce."

Ryan saw him jolt as if she had startled him out of a dream. "Ryan?" Her name on his lips was soft, questioning.

"Your front door wasn't locked, so I came in. I hope you don't mind."

He continued to stare at her and said nothing. She mounted the steps of the stage.

"I've interrupted your work."

Following her gaze, Pierce looked down at the glass vial in his hand and the colored cubes on the table.

"Work? It—no, it's all right." He set the vial down. He couldn't have managed the most basic illusion.

"This won't take long," Ryan told him with a smile. She had never seen him rattled and was all but certain she would never see him so again. "There's a new contract we need to discuss."

"Contract?" he repeated, unable to take his eyes from hers.

"Yes, that's why I've come."

"I see." He wanted to touch her but kept his hands on the table. He wouldn't touch what was no longer his. "You look well," he managed and started to offer her a chair. "Where have you been?" It was out before he could stop it; it was perilously close to an accusation. Ryan only smiled again.

"I've been away," she said simply, then took a step closer. "Have you thought of me?"

It was he who stepped back. "Yes, I've thought of you."

"Often?" The word was quiet as she moved toward him again.

"Don't Ryan!" His voice was defensively sharp as he moved back.

"I've thought of you often," she continued as if he hadn't spoken. "Constantly, though I tried not to. Do you dabble in love potions, Pierce? Is that what you did to me?" She took another step toward him. "I tried very hard to hate you and harder still to forget you. Your magic's too strong."

Her scent whirled through his senses until they were all clouded with her. "Ryan, I'm only a man, and you're my weakness. Don't do this." Pierce shook his head and called on the last of his control. "I have work to do."

Ryan glanced at the table, then toyed with one of the colored cubes. "It'll have to wait. Do you know how many hours there are in a week?" she asked and smiled at him.

"No. Stop this, Ryan." The blood was pounding in his head. The need was growing unmanageable.

"A hundred and sixty-eight," she whispered. "A lot to make up for."

"If I touch you, I won't let you go again."

"And if I touch you?" She laid her hand on his chest.

"Don't," he warned quickly. "You should leave while you still can."

"You'll do that escape again, won't you?"

"Yes. Yes, damn it." His fingertips were tingling, demanding that he reach for her. "Ryan, for God's sake, go."

"You'll do it again," she went on. "And others, probably more dangerous, or at least more frightening, because that's who you are. Isn't that what you told me?"

"Ryan—"

"That's who I fell in love with," she said calmly. "I don't know why I thought I could or should try to change that. I told you once you were exactly what I wanted, that was the truth. But I suppose I had to learn what that meant. Do you still want me, Pierce?"

He didn't answer, but she saw his eyes darken, felt his heart speed under her hand. "I can leave and have a very calm, undemanding life." Ryan took the last step to him. "Is that what you want for me? Have I hurt you so much you wish me a life of unbearable boredom? Please, Pierce," she murmured, "won't you forgive me?"

"There's nothing to forgive." He was drowning in her eyes no matter how he struggled not to. "Ryan, for the love of God!" Desperate, he pushed her hand from his chest. "Can't you see what you're doing to me?"

"Yes, and I'm so glad. I was afraid you could really shut me out." She let out a quiet sigh of relief. "I'm staying, Pierce. There's nothing you can do about it." She had her arms around his neck and her mouth a breath away from his. "Tell me again that you want me to go."

"No." He dragged her against him. "I can't." His mouth was devouring hers. Power flowed into him again, hot and painful. He pressed her closer and felt her mouth respond to the savageness of his. "It's too late," he murmured. "Much too late." Excitement was burning through him. He couldn't hold her near enough. "I won't be able to leave the door open for you now, Ryan. Do you understand?"

"Yes. Yes, I understand." She drew her head back, wanting to see his eyes. "But it'll be closed for you, too. I'm going to see to it this is one lock you can't beat."

"No escape, Ryan. For either of us." And his mouth was on hers again, hot, desperate. He felt her give against him as he crushed her to him, but her hands were strong and sure on his body. "I love you, Ryan," he told her again as he roamed her face and neck with kisses. "I love you. I lost everything when you left me."

"I won't leave you again." She took his face in her hands to stop his wandering lips. "I was wrong to ask you what I did. I was wrong to run away. I didn't trust enough."

"And now?"

"I love you, Pierce, exactly as you are."

He pulled her close again and pressed his mouth to her throat. "Beautiful Ryan, so small, so soft. God, how I want you. Come upstairs, come to bed. Let me love you properly."

Her pulses hammered at the quiet, rough words he spoke against her throat. Ryan took a deep breath, then, putting her hands on his shoulders, she pulled away. "There's the matter of a contract."

"The hell with contracts," he mumbled and tried to pull her back.

"Oh, no." Ryan stepped away from him. "I want this settled."

"I've already signed your contract," he reminded her impatiently. "Come here."

"This is a new one," she stated, ignoring him. "An exclusive life term."

He frowned. "Ryan, I'm not going to tie myself to Swan Productions for the rest of my life."

"Not Swan Productions," she countered. "Ryan Swan."

The annoyed retort on the tip of his tongue never materialized. She saw his eyes change, become intense. "What sort of contract?"

"A one-to-one, with an exclusivity clause and a lifetime term." Ryan swallowed, losing some of the confidence that had carried her this far.

"Go on."

"It's to begin immediately, with the provision of a legally binding ceremony to follow at the first reasonable opportunity." She laced her fingers together. "With a proviso for the probability of offspring." She saw Pierce's brow lift, but he said nothing. "The number of which is negotiable."

"I see," he said after a moment. "Is there a penalty clause?"

"Yes. If you try to break the terms, I'm allowed to murder you."

"Very reasonable. Your contract's very tempting, Miss Swan. What are my benefits?"

"Me."

"Where do I sign?" he asked, taking her in his arms again.

"Right here." She let out a sigh as she lifted her mouth. The kiss was gentle, promising. With a moan, Ryan drew closer.

"This ceremony, Miss Swan." Pierce nibbled at her lip as his hands began to roam. "What do you consider the first reasonable opportunity?"

"Tomorrow afternoon." She laughed and again pulled out of his arms. "You don't think I'm going to give you time to find an escape hatch, do you?"

"I've met my match, I see."

"Absolutely," she agreed with a nod. "I have a few tricks up my sleeve." Lifting the Tarot cards, she surprised Pierce by fanning them with some success. She'd been practicing for months.

"Very good." He grinned and went to her. "I'm impressed."

"You haven't seen anything yet," she promised. "Pick a card," she told him, her eyes laughing. "Any card."

*     *     *     *     *

# COMING NEXT MONTH!

If you enjoyed SUMMER DESSERTS, wait until you sample the romantic delights in Nora Roberts's LESSONS LEARNED—coming in your next shipment. It follows the story of Summer's cooking-school friend—the best and sexiest chef in Italy, Carlo Franconi.

In LESSONS LEARNED, we meet Carlo again as he is about to embark on an American tour to gain publicity for his new cookbook. Promoting Carlo's *sinfully* delicious recipes is a dream job for publicist Juliet Trent, but dealing with the outrageous Carlo is altogether different! From the moment their eyes lock together at the airport, Carlo uses his charm, his prowess in the kitchen, and his oh-so-European romanticism to win Juliet. It's a tempting combination that she finds increasingly difficult to resist....

Can Juliet stand the heat? Or should she get out of the kitchen, *fast* ...? Find out next month in LESSONS LEARNED—romance as romance should be.

THE
LANGUAGE
of LOVE